DISNEY

TALES FROM

ADVENTURELAND

THE
GOLDEN PAW

Written by Jason Lethcoe
Illustrations by Jeff Clark
Cover paint by Grace Lee
Copyright © 2018 Disney Enterprises, Inc.

Printed in the United States of America
First Hardcover Edition, April 2018
1 3 5 7 9 10 8 6 4 2
FAC-020093-18047
Library of Congress Control Number: 2016963393
ISBN 978-1-4847-8814-1

For more Disney Press fun, visit www.disneybooks.com

SUSTAINABLE FORESTRY INITIATIVE
Certified Sourcing
www.sfiprogram.org
SFI-00993
Logo Applies to Text Stock Only

DISNEY
TALES FROM

ADVENTURELAND

THE GOLDEN PAW

Jason Lethcoe

DISNEY PRESS

LOS ANGELES · NEW YORK

For Olivia Rose

Chapter One

A Calamitous Cruise!

ndy Stanley gripped the tiller of the *Nile Princess* as the ramshackle boat rocked up and down on the churning river. If anyone had told him a few months ago that he would be alone on a boat in the Congo, he would have thought they were crazy. If they had told him that he would secretly be having the time of his life, he would have thought they were talking about some other person entirely!

But here he was, battling the thundering current, his pith helmet set firmly on his head and his lips pressed together in a thin, determined line as he tried to navigate the dangerous river. His heart was pounding nearly as fast as the foaming rapids, and he could feel the sweat trickling down the back of his neck.

Andy's skinny arms ached and strained as he pushed and pulled the heavy wooden tiller back and forth, desperately trying to avoid the sharp rocks that clawed like greedy fingers at the sides of the boat. River water splashed over the front, drenching his battered brown leather jacket and plastering his blond hair to his forehead. Andy sputtered and wiped away the water from his eyes, trying to see what perils lay in front of him.

Belowdecks, Andy could hear the bilge pump whine as the machine tried to dispel the water that was filling the cabin. Faint whiffs of smoke from the overworked pump filled Andy's nostrils, and he knew it wouldn't be long before it sputtered and died.

I've got to get to land, he thought, looking around for some way to dock his boat. But it was no use. He was going too fast to stop without crashing.

As he searched desperately for somewhere safe to land, he spotted a large shape in the water just ahead of him.

What's that?

Suddenly, the gigantic object surfaced. Andy pushed hard on the tiller to avoid colliding with it. As the boat careened to the right, he swung his head to the side and saw that the object was actually the head of a mammoth hippo! The beast roared, exposing its giant canine tusks. Then, with a huge splash, it plunged back into the water and began swimming furiously after the *Nile Princess.*

"It's charging the boat!" Andy exclaimed.

But there was no one there to hear him. The entire crew was gone! For better or worse, Andy was on his own.

Andy stared at the ferocious hippo on his tail. It was faster than the boat and quickly catching up to its target. Andy may not have had a lot of experience in the water, but he knew that such a powerful animal could easily destroy the leaky ship.

His heart thudded wildly in his chest as he fumbled around, searching for anything he could use to scare the beast away. Finally, in the captain's crate, Andy spotted a flare gun.

Praying it was loaded, Andy grabbed the emergency pistol and, after nearly dropping it in his rush to get it, raised it into the air.

"Go! Get out of here!" he shouted at the huge hippo. He pulled the trigger and a bright flare leapt into the air.

Luckily, the flash of red light and the corresponding noise seemed to have an effect on the massive beast. It quickly plunged back into the murky depths of the river and began to move in the opposite direction.

"I guess you'd call that a *hippo-shot-I-miss*," Andy

mumbled under his breath, then laughed at the corny joke. It seemed his grandfather's sense of humor was starting to rub off on him.

Andy took a deep breath. His hands were trembling violently from the power of the blast, and his legs were shaking from the near collision with the hippo. He would have loved nothing more than to sit down, but the leaky boat was still splashing down the rushing river at an alarming rate. There was no time to rest.

Andy tossed the flare gun back into the crate. In spite of his shaking hands, he managed to reclaim tight control of the tiller as he tried to anticipate what other dangers might lie ahead.

The *Nile Princess* was definitely waterlogged. Andy could tell that the hull was sitting much lower in the water than when he'd first set off. The acrid smell of burning oil from the bilge pump filled the air.

There's got to be a bank or inlet somewhere that I can steer into! If I can't find one, I'm done for!

At that moment, Andy noticed a distant roar

sounding from somewhere up ahead. He paled, knowing exactly what it was.

Schweitzer Falls.

Andy been told by his guide that it was one of the deadliest and most massive waterfalls for miles around. Going over it in a sinking ship was certain doom.

Sweat broke out on Andy's forehead as the roar of the waterfall grew closer, the sound thundering all around him. Ahead of him, the river seemed to drop off in a foaming rush. All Andy could see at the edge of the falls was a horizon filled with fluffy white clouds.

CRUNCH! The waterlogged boat careened off a large boulder, and the engine, which had already been struggling, finally quit.

An eerie silence, punctuated only by the roar of the cascading falls, filled the air. Andy knew that this was it. There was no escape now. In seconds, he would tumble over the waterfall and it would all be over.

As the nose of the boat reached the edge of the precipice, Andy lunged for the nearest life preserver and prayed desperately that somehow, someway, he would survive. His last thought as the boat began to tip forward was *Maybe the Key of Fate really is cursed.*

Chapter Two
The Key of Fate

I t was supposed to be an "in-between" mission—a quick job before embarking on the search for the Golden Paw. The senior members of the Jungle Explorers' Society thought Andy could use a little more experience—a little more time in the field before setting off on a mission that was sure to stretch his abilities. It should have been easy. All he had to do was recover a key Ned had long ago hidden in the jungle.

Of course, Andy hadn't found out until the expedition

was under way that the mysterious Key of Fate he was being sent to retrieve was rumored to be cursed. According to Jack McGraw, the leader of the expedition, great danger and calamity would befall anyone who possessed it. But still, Andy was the Keymaster, and securing the key was his responsibility.

What nobody in the Society had counted on was the fact that the key had fallen into the possession of a troop of angry gorillas, and that retrieving it would put several members of the Society in serious danger! Andy could still picture the look of terror on Jack McGraw's face as he and the three other navigation experts had clung to the top of a palm tree, an angry rhino snorting beneath them.

Andy had known he had to save his friends!

"Hey! Leave them alone!" he'd shouted, trying to make his voice sound as loud and authoritative as possible. Apparently, it had been enough to get the rhino's attention, for the great beast had turned and leveled its beady eyes directly at him.

As the rhino had snorted and pawed the ground with a huge hoof, preparing to attack, Andy had quickly pulled out his Zoomwriter fountain pen and pointed it at the beast.

The fountain pen, which was not only a rare and wonderful writing device but had also been modified to be a weapon, was Andy's saving grace. It had been a gift from Andy's grandfather, the great Ned Lostmore.

Andy had leveled his pen and aimed its explosive pulse at the rhino. It worked! The rhino flew backward. But the sound of the blast drew the attention of the nearby gorillas, who had been slowly gathering around the palm tree. The group had turned to Andy and begun howling and thumping their massive chests. Andy hadn't wasted any time. He'd fired his Zoomwriter a second time.

But that time, he'd missed.

The next thing Andy had known, a stampede of angry gorillas was charging at him.

Andy had been so intent on his own survival that

he hadn't heard the shouts of instruction from his treed colleagues. Deep down, part of him had wondered if he should be running away. He was trying to qualify to become a full member of the Jungle Explorers' Society. Weren't they supposed to stand and fight? But at the time, he'd been too scared to consider the thought.

Fortunately for the young Keymaster, he had managed to hang on to the goal of the expedition, the pitted brass key he'd been sent to recover.

Just save the key, Andy remembered thinking as he ran away. *That's what's most important. The others can take care of themselves.*

Andy had just barely made it to the boat. As he shoved off from the dock and leapt aboard, he'd narrowly missed being grabbed by the fastest of the ferocious gorillas.

Now, as he tipped over Schweitzer Falls, Andy wondered how everything had gone so wrong, and how he could possibly survive this situation.

Chapter Three
Happy Meetings

The answer to his prayers appeared out of nowhere. If Andy had had time to think, he would have thought that Abigail Awol—determined expression on her face and braided hair flying behind her like a banner as she gripped a long rope and flew toward him—looked like a heroine out of a movie. But instead, the only thought Andy had time for as Abigail grabbed him around the waist and yanked him to safety was relief at the fact that he'd somehow been spared.

And that she couldn't have come at a better time.

As the two scrabbled onto a nearby bank, Andy tried not to retch. Gathering himself, he turned to Abigail and offered her a shaky smile.

"That was really good timing," he said.

Abigail laughed. "You're telling me! You wouldn't *believe* how fast I had to run to get to the falls before you did. I think I might have set some kind of world record!"

Andy edged toward the rocky bank and peered over the cliff. His boat had smashed to pieces on the rocks far, far below.

"It seems like saying thank you is hardly enough," Andy said as he quickly stepped back from the edge. The sight of his shattered boat and the thought that he had very nearly been aboard it was making him feel nauseated. "You saved my life!"

"I'm sure you'd do the same," Abigail replied with a shrug. "It's what a Jungle Explorers' Society member does, right?"

"Right," Andy said. But even as he uttered the words, his heart sank. The fact that he'd been the one rescued and not doing the rescuing was sure to be noted by the others. And, inwardly, Andy wondered if he could have pulled off such a bold and incredible rescue.

Abigail was the daughter of Albert Awol, Ned Lostmore's oldest friend and a great adventurer in his own right. His daughter had definitely inherited her father's bravery. Andy sighed as he thought about the cowardice he had shown in leaving the members of his team behind. His grandfather kept telling him he had the Lostmore Spirit, but right now it felt like Abigail had a lot more of it than he did.

"Come on," Abigail said. "I'll take you to base camp. It's not too far from here."

As Andy walked with Abigail through the deep undergrowth, he explained what had happened with the gorillas.

"But you got the key, right?" Abigail asked.

Andy grinned and patted his right trouser pocket.

"Right here." Then Andy's expression grew troubled. "I hope the others made it to safety."

His hand remained on the key in his pocket. He hoped that having retrieved it would be enough to redeem him for his botched mission.

Andy was so deep in thought that he didn't notice when Abigail stopped moving. "Oof," he said, crashing into her.

Abigail raised her finger to her lips and gripped Andy's arm. "There's something moving out there," she whispered.

Andy scanned the dense jungle and listened intently. He didn't see or hear anything amiss.

After a few moments of standing in silence, Andy whispered, "I don't hear anything. Maybe it's a false—"

But he never got to the word *alarm*. Without warning, a gigantic shape leapt, snarling, from behind a tree.

"Down!" Abigail shouted.

Andy fell to the ground as Abigail pushed down hard on his shoulder. A flash of tawny fur with ebony stripes shot over him. Andy whirled around to see Abigail standing face to face with a giant tiger! And judging by the pronounced ribs on its heaving flanks, it was very hungry.

"Nice kitty," Abigail said in a soothing voice. "We don't want to hurt you."

I think she's got it the wrong way around, Andy thought. He reached slowly into his pocket, trying not to make any sudden moves. Carefully, he removed his Zoomwriter and twisted the cap.

I hope the battery has had some time to charge.

The tiger drooled as it stalked closer to Abigail, its body tensed and ready to spring. Andy knew he had to work fast. Everything depended on his being able to distract the beast with his pen.

Andy pressed the top of the cap, aiming the pen directly at the massive cat.

When completely full, the pen could have easily knocked the beast back at least fifty feet. However, it hadn't had enough time to fully recharge. But it wasn't completely dead. The pen had just enough power left to produce a very large *BANG!*

With a hiss that sounded as loud as a steam engine, the beast leapt into the air, its tail stiff, and bolted into the nearby brush.

Andy's hand shook as he lowered the Zoomwriter.

Abigail offered him a grateful smile. "Good thinking!" she said.

"Th-thanks," stuttered Andy as he placed the pen back in his pocket. Then, keeping his eyes peeled and his footfalls as soft as possible, he followed Abigail the rest of the way to the camp.

Andy's eyes widened as he looked around at the sophisticated base camp. The hastily cleared plot of land was dotted with portable bungalows. A large fire pit in the center of camp was equipped with a cooking station, and the delicious smells of roasted plantains, pork, and freshly brewed coffee filled the air. Several Society members were gathered around the fire, sitting on camp chairs and sipping from metal cups. Andy recognized the curling red mustache of his friend Rusty Bucketts, a bush pilot with a shiny ball bearing in place of his missing eye. Andy had seen firsthand how accurate a weapon Rusty's artificial eye and trusty slingshot could be. The pilot was hot-tempered but good-natured, and Andy was glad to see that he was part of the team.

Sitting next to the pilot were the beautiful conjoined twins, Betty and Dotty. The sisters were lethal assassins and martial arts experts, as lovely and deadly as poisonous flowers. When they saw Andy, the two flashed him matching delighted smiles. Andy offered a wave and smiled back, blushing a little at the attention.

Andy glanced around the camp for anyone else he might know. He had met many of the Society members during his last mission. But Molly the talkative mime and Cedric the witch doctor weren't in sight. Abigail's father, Albert, seemed to be absent as well.

"I wonder where they are," Andy murmured. "I was really hoping to see them again."

Before Andy could think any further on where his missing friends might be, his eyes alighted on a familiar figure standing a little apart from the others. It was a big barrel-chested robot with a heavy glass plate on its torso. Andy recognized his grandfather's robotic assistant, Boltonhouse, at once. More importantly, he recognized the precious cargo the machine carried in its transparent chest cavity.

"Grandfather!" Andy exclaimed, running over to greet him.

Bobbing on a string inside the robot's rotund metal chest was Dr. Ned Lostmore, a living, breathing shrunken head.

Ned chuckled when he saw his grandson. "Andy, my boy! You made it. Knew you would, of course," Ned said in his sophisticated English accent. Andy saw that Ned's blue eyes were twinkling and his white handlebar mustache was turned upward with his broad, welcoming smile. "And the key?" Ned asked.

"It wasn't easy, but I got it," Andy said, producing

the key he'd been sent to retrieve. Ned squinted through his monocle at the brass key and nodded with satisfaction.

"Well done, lad. Well done, indeed! That particular key has given us a deuce of a time. It opens a very special vault. If it hadn't been for the disastrous run-in that led to my current, ahem, *disembodied* state, I feel certain that I would have never misplaced such a valuable object. It's difficult to complete a mission when one has a shrunken head and no body."

"The gorillas didn't seem too happy to give it up," Andy said. "I think they liked how shiny it was."

"Egad! Gorillas? You don't say!"

"I do say," Andy said with a laugh. "The key fell into the possession of a group of angry gorillas. I nearly died trying to get it away from them. Do you know how fast they are? Not to mention that rhino. . . ."

Instead of being horrified by Andy's experience, Ned seemed delighted by the adventure. "Ha! The more dangerous the adventure the better the story, what?

That old Lostmore Spirit kept you on your toes. Nothing like a good escape to get one's blood pumping, eh?"

"Well, I can think of other safer ways," Andy admitted, feeling relieved. It seemed that his grandfather wasn't blaming him for the mission going so wrong.

"You look pale, my boy," Ned said, squinting at Andy through the glass. "I suggest you take a tonic made from strawberries, raspberries, snaggleberries, and cherries. Guaranteed to restore a bit of color to your cheeks, what?"

Andy shrugged. "If you say so."

"By Jove, what happened to the rest of the expedition?" Ned asked, seeming to notice for the first time that Andy was alone. "Where's Jack McGraw?"

"Um," Andy said awkwardly, "I . . . I'm not sure. The last time I saw him, he and the others were trapped in a tree by a rhino."

"And you left them behind?" Ned, who had seemed jolly up until that point, leveled a serious gaze at Andy. "Tut-tut! The first rule of the Jungle Explorers' Society is that no member is ever left behind. Jack McGraw is critical to this particular mission. How could you have done such a thing?"

Andy blushed and lowered his head. It was what he'd feared would happen. Just getting the key back wasn't enough. *How* he'd gotten it seemed to be equally important. The Society expected its members to display courage and integrity. Deep down, Andy had known he should have stayed to help Jack and the others rather than run for the boat.

Ned looked at his embarrassed grandson and sighed. "Chin up, lad. Everyone makes mistakes. You'll have other chances to prove yourself."

Andy nodded. He was determined to try again at the first opportunity. "What's this about an old vault?" he asked, changing the subject back to the Key of Fate. "What's inside of it?"

Ned lowered his voice into a conspiratorial whisper. "Only the greatest book ever written. Inside the vault is a tome from the ancient Library of Alexandria, the only book to survive the fire that destroyed the largest collection of historical knowledge in the world. What is written in that single volume would change the way you think about everything, my dear boy. Everything! The fate of the world relies on the vault's never being opened. . . ."

Ned's voice trailed off and Andy saw the faraway look in his grandfather's eyes. Then Ned shook himself, bobbing on the string that held him suspended inside his glass container. He called up to the mechanical man: "Boltonhouse, take the key from Andy."

The robot extended a hand and grabbed the key from Andy's outstretched palm.

Andy's grandfather gave him a wink and said, "Why don't you join the others by the fire? I've some important business to attend to, namely making absolutely certain that this key doesn't go missing again."

Then, with an abrupt turn, Boltonhouse marched toward the largest of the bungalows. Andy stared after his departing grandfather for a moment before turning with a shrug and walking over to where the others were gathered.

I wonder where he's planning on taking that key. As the Keymaster, I thought I would be responsible for its safekeeping.

But Andy had learned not to question his grandfather's ways. As the leader of the secret society, Ned decided what needed to be done.

Andy grinned as he greeted his companions, and after a welcoming cup of tea and plate of food were shoved into his hands, they all demanded to hear about his expedition.

By the flickering light of the fire, Andy chronicled his harrowing encounter. When he got to the part about running to the boat alone, there was an awkward silence. Thankfully, Abigail interrupted the embarrassing moment by telling the stories of how Andy had scared off the hippo from the leaking boat and of her daring rescue at the edge of the falls.

As the others slapped Abigail on the back, praising

her for coming to Andy's aid, Andy felt a renewed sense of shame.

Next time, I'll *be the one doing the rescuing*, he thought determinedly. *I just hope they'll give me another chance.*

Chapter Four

The Expedition Team

The next morning, Andy awoke feeling completely disoriented. He'd been dreaming that he was back on the *Nile Princess*, only this time, instead of facing a waterfall, he'd been surrounded by swarms of crocodiles, all chomping at the sides of his boat as he desperately tried to fight them off with nothing but a limp strand of spaghetti.

It sounded silly now that he was awake, but it had made for a restless night, and Andy couldn't stop yawning at breakfast. His tousled thatch of blond hair stood up in even more of a haystack than usual, and Abigail giggled the moment he sat down.

"I don't know what's so funny," Andy said grumpily.

"You look like you've been in a hurricane," she said. "You want to borrow my comb?"

"You sound like my mother," Andy said, running his hand through his hair. "Trust me, it won't help."

Andy had just finished a rather bland bowl of oatmeal when Rusty stood and banged on the side of his tin cup with a spoon, calling the group to attention.

"All right, let's get started," he boomed. "We've quite a bit of material to cover and I'd like your full attention." He narrowed his gaze at Betty and Dotty, who were deep in conversation about various poisonous plants and their antidotes. The two glanced up, obviously irritated at the interruption. The sisters glared at Rusty, then both sighed at the same time. With a flick of her finger, Betty gestured for Rusty to continue.

"Thank you, ladies. Rest assured, what I have to say won't keep you from discussing ways to kill your enemies for too long."

Andy listened closely as Rusty began to outline the latest quest.

"As you all know, we've been searching for some time now for a cursed artifact called the Golden Paw. Our intelligence tells us that the Collective is searching for this artifact as well, and are on track to find it before we do if we don't act immediately."

"The Collective?" Andy asked. "Who are they?"

"We don't know much about their members," Rusty explained. "Just that they are an assembled group of the worst criminals around. Phink was one of them, but his secrets died with him. They keep their membership secret. The one thing we do know is that their leader, the Potentate, is directing their efforts."

"What about the artifact? What does it actually do?" Andy asked.

"The paw?" Rusty replied. "Legend says that it can confound the bearer's enemies, allowing the person who possesses it to magically take on any appearance they desire. They can make themselves look like a person's best friend or family member—even a king or queen." Rusty sighed and then continued, looking troubled. "The implications of using such an artifact are boundless. The legend also states that the paw was designed for evil purposes, and as such, extracts a heavy price from the person who uses it, shortening their lifespan considerably. Every minute the user spends impersonating another is another minute taken from their own existence. Only someone truly evil would use such a cursed object."

Andy's mind reeled, thinking over the possibilities. A person could do a lot of damage with such a thing. Maybe even take over the world!

"Until recently, the Golden Paw was thought to be a myth," Rusty continued. "But if what we have heard is true and they have nearly found its location, then we must take it as fact that it exists. More than that, if the Collective wants it, we must assume that they will waste no time in trying to retrieve it."

Andy felt a nervous fluttering in his stomach as Rusty continued.

"Ned will remain here, gathering whatever intel he can on our enemy's position. In the meantime, he's provided me with the fastest route to the location where the Golden Paw is rumored to be hidden and has asked that I assemble a team to beat the Collective to its whereabouts."

As Rusty narrowed his one good eye and gazed around at the group, Andy found himself desperately hoping that he would get to go. He had come a long way from the boy he used to be, a boy who would rather have read about adventure in a book than actually partake in one. But after the way he'd bungled the last mission, he worried that he might be forced to sit this one out.

Pick me, please, pick me.

"Betty, Dotty, you'll both be needed for this," Rusty said.

"As if one of us could stay behind," Dotty murmured to her twin sister with a roll of her eyes.

Rusty continued, ignoring the sisters. His gaze alighted on Abigail and he grinned. "Feeling up for another one, Abigail?"

Andy watched as the girl leapt to her feet and saluted. "Ready when you are, Captain Bucketts!"

Rusty laughed and nodded. "At ease, soldier!"

The group all gave Abigail congratulatory pats on the back for being included in the expedition. Until recently, Abigail had been a member of the Collective, the very group they were fighting against. But she had turned her back on the organization and done her part to help Andy fulfill his last mission. Now she was trying to prove her worth and commitment to the Jungle Explorers' Society. The others had understandably been treating her with a bit of guarded suspicion, but Andy had watched as she'd made good on all her promises over the last few months, and the fact that she'd rescued him the day before had evidently put her in good standing.

He couldn't help feeling just a little bit jealous that she'd been picked.

"Ordinarily, Molly and Albert would round out the team, but Molly is on a mission in Paris and Albert is working with Ned to find out more about the Golden Paw. That means, in addition to Abigail, we'll need one more." He paused, as if considering whether he'd made the right decision. He was just about to speak up again when a loud voice rang out. . . .

"Ho there, hope I'm not intruding! Charlie, get a shot of me next to the big guy. . . ."

A man in a dazzling white safari outfit, complete with matching pith helmet, strode into the assembly. Next to him was a pudgy man with a motion picture camera, cranking a handle and capturing everything on film.

"Right, J.B. I'm on it. . . ."

As Charlie swung the camera around and pointed

it at Rusty, the man in the white suit strode over to the stunned bush pilot and shook his hand. When he smiled, revealing two rows of perfect white teeth and a strong-jawed profile, Andy gasped.

It's John Bartlemore, the actor! I can't believe it!

Chapter Five

An Unexpected Visitor

Andy had seen John Bartlemore in countless adventure serials, always playing the part of Dan Daring, an intrepid jungle explorer and treasure hunter. The *Dan Daring* serials were a favorite of most boys his age, and the show often featured fantastic creatures like Egyptian mummies and fearsome gorillas. Now that Andy had seen such creatures for himself, he realized just how unrealistic the suits the actors wore looked.

A whispered buzz rippled around the assembly as the others recognized the actor, too. The only one not impressed was Rusty, who seemed quite put out that the unexpected visitor had stumbled upon their secret meeting.

"And who in the blazes are you?" Rusty asked, dropping the hand that Bartlemore was pumping furiously.

"What? You don't know who I am? That's priceless! Are you getting all this, Charlie?" Bartlemore replied, evidently enjoying himself. "He doesn't know who I am!"

"Got it, J.B.," replied his cameraman.

"You're John Bartlemore!" exclaimed Abigail. She blushed furiously as the handsome actor turned to her and grinned.

"That's me! We were on a shoot in the area and spotted your little . . . er . . . gathering," he said brightly as he motioned vaguely to the tents. "And who are you, lovely lady, and what are you folks doing here? Is it some kind of campout?"

Andy couldn't help noticing that Abigail turned an even deeper shade of crimson when Bartlemore called her "lovely lady."

"Abigail Awol," she replied softly. "I've seen all of your movies." She gazed at the actor with what Andy thought were almost literal stars in her eyes.

Suddenly, the arrival of one of his silver screen heroes didn't seem so great. Andy had never seen Abigail, who was usually supremely confident, act like one of those giggling, prissy girls he'd seen at school who spent all day mooning over the celebrity gossip magazines.

Who does he think he is, barging in on us like this? Andy thought. *These Hollywood types think that they own the world!*

From the look on Rusty's face, it seemed the pilot must be thinking about the same thing. Rusty's face had turned bright red, and Andy knew that it wasn't from embarrassment. His red mustache bristled and his one good eye glared at Bartlemore, looking every bit as steely as his fake one.

"Listen, Mr. Bartlemore. We're a team of highly trained research scientists on an archaeological expedition. I'm sorry we can't accommodate visitors right now, but we're working here," he said through gritted teeth. "If you don't mind . . ."

"Archaeologists? Well, that's just splendid!" Bartlemore said, rubbing his hands together. "Searching for lost treasure, eh? That's just the thing that would get me the front page of the trades. Hey, Charlie, can you believe my luck?"

"Great luck, J.B. Couldn't be luckier," replied the cameraman. Andy noticed that he was still filming.

Bartlemore snapped his fingers and his Hollywood smile grew even bigger. "I've got it! We'll film all this and put it in a newsreel in front of my next picture." He gestured to the group. "You'll all be famous!" He wiggled his eyebrows. "Who wouldn't like a bit of fame and fortune, eh? Well, maybe not *fortune*. . . . That part belongs to me. Hah!"

Andy noticed that instead of exciting them,

Bartlemore's news made everyone nervous. The cover story Rusty had come up with was fine as long as they all remained anonymous. But for most of them, being a part of the Jungle Explorers' Society was supposed to be a secret. They couldn't afford to have their faces splashed across every movie screen in America.

How arrogant can a person be? Andy wondered. *He thinks that because he's famous, we'll just do what he says?*

"Sorry, no," said Rusty.

But Bartlemore didn't appear to be listening. He was busy telling Charlie to get a shot of him standing next to Betty and Dotty. The sisters glared at the actor, and Andy knew that if he wasn't careful, it might be Bartlemore who ended up a headline in the papers back home.

Actor found dead in jungle. Cause of death: mysterious razor-sharp throwing stars.

Even as he thought it, Andy could see Betty fingering the pouch at her belt.

Abigail must have seen it, too, and ran over to where Bartlemore was standing with his arm around Dotty's shoulders.

"Mr. Bartlemore, I'm truly sorry, but this is not a good time," Abigail said. "As wonderful as your offer is, I'm afraid we must decline."

Abigail flashed him a beautiful smile, but Bartlemore just stared back at her with a confused expression.

"Decline? Well . . . that's . . . that's quite unexpected." He struck a theatrical thinking pose, his finger perched on his dimpled jaw and his other hand on his hip. "Quite unexpected. Did you hear that, Charlie? They are declining our very generous offer."

"I heard, J.B. Declined the offer. A stupid move, J.B.," Charlie said.

"I agree, Charlie. Quite stupid," replied Bartlemore. He turned back to Abigail and put his big hand on her shoulder. The expression he wore was one that looked as if he were explaining something profound to a very simpleminded student.

"Thank you for your opinion, lovely lady. But I'm afraid declining is not an option. I've decided. We will be coming with you folks, whether you like it or not."

Abigail stared at him in disbelief. It wasn't the answer she'd expected.

It was all too much for Rusty. The man snorted like an enraged bull and marched over to Bartlemore, looking as if he'd like to tear the man limb from limb.

"Now see here!" he shouted.

But Bartlemore merely turned to him, a calm expression on his face. "No, *you* see. There's no law prohibiting me from following you through this jungle. You can't stop me. I have attorneys back in Los Angeles who would slap you with a lawsuit so fast it would make your head spin."

Bartlemore turned and took a deep breath, smelling the jungle air and looking around as if he owned the entire thing.

"I'm going to enjoy this. Come on, Charlie, let's get back to camp. I've got some ideas for the script."

"Coming, J.B.," Charlie said, and ignoring the stunned expressions on the faces of Rusty and the rest of the explorers, the cameraman marched dutifully after his boss without ever taking his eye away from the camera lens.

Andy walked over to Rusty, who was staring furiously at the tree-lined spot where they'd disappeared.

"What should we do?" Andy asked.

Rusty paused and then replied with a dangerous-looking smile, "Let him follow. There's no way a two-bit Hollywood actor could possibly survive the mission we're about to undertake."

Rusty glanced down at Andy and added, in a gruff voice, "You're going, too. If it were up to me you'd stay behind, but Ned's orders are Ned's orders. Pack your kit."

As Andy, feeling both exhilarated that he was going and worried that something terrible was going to happen, ran back to his tent to get his things, he couldn't help thinking *Bartlemore is about to find out just how unlike the movies adventures really are!*

Chapter Six

Escape by Night

The following morning, the group woke extra early. "All the more difficult for Bartlemore" was the phrase Rusty had coined the night before, and Andy had found that since then he had taken to using it often.

The trouble is, what's difficult for Bartlemore is also difficult for us! Andy thought as he washed up in a steel bucket. It was so dark he could barely see the towel next to his canteen, and he nearly grabbed a bunch of mosquito netting to dry his face.

Andy's eyelids felt like they had weights tied to them as he shouldered his heavy rucksack and began the trek through the jungle to the airport where, Rusty had said, they would receive further instructions. As he walked, Andy patted his pocket. Thankfully, he'd remembered to bring his Zoomwriter. He'd nearly forgotten it in his rush to leave the tent.

Not having my pen would be a disaster, he thought. How could he ever succeed in his big second chance if he couldn't defend himself?

Besides, not only was the fountain pen weapon incredibly handy, but he was an avid collector of writing instruments. Who knew if he'd be coming back to this base camp? He never would have forgiven himself if he'd left it behind and not been able to get it back.

The group walked quietly, trying to make as little noise as possible. "All the more difficult for Bartlemore," Rusty had whispered.

Andy hazarded a look over his shoulder. There was no sign that they were being followed.

Bartlemore's probably snoring away under a cash-mere blanket right now.

Andy smirked. A Hollywood actor like Bartlemore finding it in himself to get up before noon was probably impossible. Andy had heard that the rich and famous had it pretty easy.

He's in for quite a shock when he finds out that we already left. I wonder what he'll say to his cameraman about that.

The thought of an outraged Bartlemore perked him up a little as he followed Rusty down a winding path. The brush was thick, but the big pilot easily led the way, cutting swaths of undergrowth with his razor-sharp machete, hardly making a sound as he went.

The group zigged and zagged through the jungle in what Andy assumed was an effort to thwart any attempt by Bartlemore to follow them. It might take twice as long to get to wherever it was that they were going, but Andy was content to follow Rusty's lead.

As the darkness gradually began to lift, Andy took

in his surroundings. Tall fruit trees grew everywhere, their long, hairy vines dangling like tentacles from their heavy branches. The trees were much easier to handle when they weren't smacking your face in the darkness, conjuring up images of pythons. Andy had nearly jumped out of his boots when the first one had grazed his cheek and had spent the next five minutes unconsciously brushing the side of his face at just the thought of the huge snakes.

Finally, after hours of marching, Rusty's big voice boomed out, "Ah, there it is!"

Andy looked up. The tall trees had come to an abrupt end, and a wide swath of land had been cleared for a large wooden building with a huge tower.

"The Jungle Navigation Company Airport," Rusty said with a smile. "Spent many weeks at this place when I was in training as a bush pilot. Good times!"

Upon closer inspection, Andy could make out a runway with a few shabby planes parked nearby. A tattered wind sock, a hollow fabric tube mounted to a bamboo pole for the purposes of indicating the direction of the wind, fluttered on top of the tower, and the faintest sound of big band music drifted on the breeze.

Rusty glanced back down the pathway in the direction from which they'd come. "Let's just see him try to follow us," he grunted. Then, adjusting his pack, he led the way down to the airport.

Chapter Seven
The Airport

There was no possible way Andy could have been prepared for what he saw when he entered the airport. Even an army of gorillas or a giant crocodile would have surprised him less.

Battered and sweaty from the long jungle hike, the group emerged into the clearing—only to find a clean-shaven Bartlemore lounging in a hammock waiting for them. His sycophantic cameraman, Charlie, sat in a chair beside him.

Bartlemore leapt from the hammock and grinned. "About time!" he exclaimed. "Took you long enough to get here. Charlie, are you ready to roll?"

Charlie shouldered his camera and gazed through the eyepiece. "Ready to go, J.B."

Andy could hardly speak. The only word that left his mouth was a small whispered *"How?"*

"We were intending to follow you, but instead, you followed us," Bartlemore said, grinning. "Leaving at the crack of dawn. Tricky." He waggled a finger at Rusty. "But the fact is, I already knew where you were off to. We used the studio plane to beat you here."

Bartlemore smiled again at the confused look on Rusty's face. "Oh, the studio plowed a landing field about a mile from your campsite months ago. And since this is the only real airport for miles around, we assumed this was where you were going. No other way to get out of the jungle, unless you want to go back upstream or over the waterfall."

Bartlemore laid his hand on Rusty's shoulder and

gave him a sympathetic look. "If you'd only asked, I'd have been happy to arrange travel for your little group on the plane. There's plenty of space. My producer spared no expense on this little junket, and we have a fridge stocked with champagne and beluga caviar."

He gazed down at Rusty's travel-stained shirt and ripped shorts. "Might have saved you a cleaning bill, too."

Rusty looked like he was about to explode. He shoved Bartlemore's hand off his shoulder and stalked toward the door to the wooden building. Andy and the others quickly followed, glaring at Bartlemore as they passed.

Inside, Rusty bolted the door. The bush pilot gritted his teeth but didn't say a word as he led the group past a row of battered desks with typewriters. Andy and Abigail exchanged worried glances. Rusty seemed really angry. Angrier than either of them had ever seen him before.

At the back of the room was another door that led to

a spiral staircase. The group silently climbed the steps. At the top, Andy gazed around at a panoramic view of the jungle.

This must be the control tower, he mused. Andy peered through the nearest pane of glass at the runway below. Then, looking around the large square room, he spotted a desk next to a bay filled with countless switches and buttons. A microphone and headset rested on the desk, and there was a faded picture of Queen Victoria on the wall.

Suddenly, a door banged open and a very harried-looking woman entered the room.

"You're late! I was afraid something might have happened. Who's that fellow with the funny-looking cameraman outside? His plane landed a few hours ago . . . an Armstrong Whitworth European twin engine. Very nice! You know him?"

Andy noticed that the whole time the woman was speaking, she was smacking a piece of gum. Her blond hair was up in a fashionable bun, but her face was freckled and rather plain except for her lipstick, which was a startling pink. She wore a leather pilot's jacket and high boots.

The woman noticed the others staring at her and introduced herself.

"Where are my manners? Yaw Ripcord," she said, shaking everyone's hand in turn. Andy noticed that she had a very firm grip.

"When I'm not piloting a plane, I'm the local dispatcher for all the flights coming in and out of the jungle. Not that we get a ton of traffic, but when we do"—she paused to pop her gum with a loud *CRACK!*—"I'm the gal who gets the job done."

Without waiting for the others to introduce themselves, she wheeled back around to Rusty. "So? What kept you?"

Rusty's eyes narrowed. "That idiot downstairs is an actor from Hollywood who's following us. How quickly can you get us airborne? Did Ned send you a communiqué?"

Yaw patted the pocket of her flight jacket. "Got it this morning. First stop, Iquitos, Peru? He said that by the time we get to our destination in Cuzco, he should have complete mission instructions waiting for you."

She cocked her head and, after blowing a bubble, asked, "So what's this all about, Bucketts?"

"You know I can't discuss Society business, Yaw. Ned keeps you on retainer for special circumstances, and we're in a pretty *special* one right now."

Andy noticed him looking out the window toward the clearing where they'd left Bartlemore. "The sooner we can get in the air, the better."

"Cagey as always. Well, surprise, surprise, this time your boss asked me if I would join you as official pilot and guide for the expedition . . . said you would be too busy to fly. Paid a pretty penny, too, I might add," she said with a wink.

Rusty looked surprised. But his expression quickly turned from concern into a grin. "Well, he couldn't have gotten anyone more qualified." Rusty turned to the group and gestured toward Yaw with his thumb.

"Ripcord here went to piloting school with me. Top of the class! Although I did give you a run for your money on that medical run to New Guinea. Beat you there and back with thirty minutes to spare."

"Twenty-nine," Yaw corrected with a smile. "Come on, let's get aboard. I want to hear all about your motley crew and Mr. Fancy Pants downstairs. I feel like I've seen him somewhere before."

Yaw turned toward a door Andy hadn't noticed before. *"Louie!"* she shouted.

There was a muffled reply from somewhere behind the wall.

"Take over the tower. I'm off!"

"You got it, boss!"

Yaw turned to Rusty. "Ready?"

Rusty nodded. "The sooner we can get away from Bartlemore, the better," he said. Then, with a nod and a wave, he gestured for the rest of the group to follow.

As they walked back down the stairs, Andy moved

next to Abigail and whispered, "What do you think? Can we get out of here without Bartlemore following us this time?"

Abigail shrugged. "Fat chance," she said.

But Andy couldn't help noticing that when she said it, it wasn't with the same negative feeling the others seemed to carry toward the Hollywood actor. It seemed like she wasn't too upset at the idea of Dan Daring's following them. In fact, it seemed like she might even *like* the idea. And knowing that made Andy like John Bartlemore even less than he already did.

Chapter Eight
Gone in a Flash

Yaw Ripcord got them up in the air within ten minutes. But it wasn't fast enough to shake Bartlemore. Within an hour, Yaw received a radio message from Louie that Bartlemore's plane was following them.

"His plane is much bigger than mine," she shouted to the group over the roar of the propellers. "It's going to be hard to shake him."

"Do your best," Rusty replied. He was sitting next to Yaw in the cockpit and functioning as her copilot.

Andy and the others were sitting in the cabin. Their seats had been modified with comfortable cushions and old-fashioned upholstery. In fact, the entire interior of the plane seemed more like someone's living room than an airplane.

Betty and Dotty noticed Andy examining a china plate with a puppy painted on it that was fastened to the cabin wall.

"I've heard that Yaw lives on the plane when she's not working in the tower. That she's got a bunk in the luggage compartment. She loves planes so much, I wouldn't be surprised if it were true," Betty said.

Andy raised his eyebrows in surprise. "That would explain why it feels so homey in here. Funny, at first glance she doesn't seem like a person who would like all this kind of . . ." He gestured to the floral-printed chairs and silk flowers on a small dining table.

"Froufrou?" Betty asked. She laughed. "We've known

her for years, and as tough as she seems on the outside, Yaw still has a softer side. When she's not fixing the motor on her plane, she likes to do needlepoint."

Andy grinned.

"Why do you think we're going to Iquitos?" Abigail asked. "What's waiting for us in Peru?"

"We've arranged to meet Cedric there," Dotty explained. "And since the Jungle Explorers' Society has one of its main office headquarters in Cuzco, I assume we'll be in touch with Ned Lostmore once we arrive to find out more about our mission."

Betty nodded and chimed in. "For now, you two should get some rest. Peru is more than six thousand miles away, and it's going to take a while to get there. Once we land, we won't have much time for rest. You might wish you'd taken advantage of the time to sleep."

Andy noticed something interesting: instead of chairs, the sisters were situated on a comfy-looking sofa. Betty smiled and handed him one of the pillows that was next to the armrest.

"This plane seems pretty small. Will we have enough fuel to get there? What if we run out? Are there stops along the way?" Andy asked. He knew that traveling such distances usually required much larger passenger planes. But his question went unanswered. Betty and Dotty had already settled into the couch and lowered silken sleeping masks over their eyes. Abigail saw Andy's nervous expression and laid a hand on his shoulder.

"Relax, Andy. The J.E.S. has waypoints between here and there for refueling. Yaw knows what she's doing. My dad told me about her. She's worked with the Society for years."

Andy nodded. He was a planner by nature and liked to know all the facts about everything before diving in. Unfortunately for him, he was coming to realize that his grandfather Ned wasn't like that at all. Ned preferred figuring things out on the go.

Andy sighed and decided that he'd try to follow the sisters' advice. He pulled his leather jacket over himself like a blanket and tried lowering his battered newsboy cap over his eyes. But as he leaned back in his chair and closed his eyes, his mind kept wandering to Bartlemore, the fact that their enemies had a head start, what exactly the Golden Paw was, and whether they could find it first.

Stop thinking! he told himself. *All you need to worry about is the here and now. The rest will figure itself out.*

But try as he might, it was several hours before Andy finally fell asleep. And when he did, his mind was filled with troubled dreams.

Chapter Nine
The Fueling Station

Andy was awakened by a heavy thud as the landing gear of Yaw's twin-engine plane touched the ground. The cabin was dark, but he saw glimpses of light speeding by outside the windows and then slowing as the air brakes were applied.

When the plane finally shuddered to a stop, he yawned hugely and glanced around at the others. Betty and Dotty were quietly snoring in unison, seemingly unaware that the plane had stopped. Abigail was curled up in a ball, her legs tucked under her on the cushy seat next to him. Andy hesitated, then lightly touched her shoulder and shook it gently.

"Wake up, Abigail," he whispered. "We've landed."

The girl raised her head and squinted at him. "It's probably just a fuel stop. Go back to sleep."

But now that Andy was awake, a strong desire to get off the plane and stretch his legs overcame him. He quietly unbuckled his seat belt and, moving as quietly as he could, made his way toward the front of the plane.

The door next to the cockpit was open, and Rusty and Yaw were nowhere to be seen. Andy cautiously stepped through and onto the collapsible stairway.

The air outside was warm and rather muggy. Andy could see that they were parked next to a long thatched hut with a large fuel truck next to it. Torches illuminated a sign painted in large block letters that read TRADER SAM'S FOOD AND FUEL.

Andy couldn't remember the last time he'd eaten. His stomach growled and he made his way down the stairs toward the hut, wondering if they had a candy bar or something.

If they do, I'll pick up one for Abigail, too, he thought.

Andy pulled open the rickety bamboo door and stepped inside. The interior of Trader Sam's was lit with a string of ship's lanterns that cast a warm glow over everything in the shop. The place was kind of dusty, and the shelves were crammed with all kinds of knick-knacks and souvenirs. On a rack near the front of the store were several handmade postcards, each depicting a watercolor painting of the Amazon River with various animals and birds.

These are pretty good, Andy thought. The illustrations were expertly done and were priced at just a nickel. He picked out one of a happy-looking water buffalo and wandered deeper into the store, searching for a snack area.

He passed several carved masks and wooden chests, the kind that a pirate might use to bury treasure. There were ships in bottles and tin lamps, tattered books and tiger skins. Everything looked fascinating, and he couldn't help examining each item and wondering how it had ended up in the shop. Had they been scavenged from shipwrecks? Or did this mysterious Trader Sam get shipments flown in from somewhere?

Judging from the amount of dust, he must not sell very much, Andy mused.

Finally, Andy found a shelf filled with what he was looking for: rows of candy bars, with names he didn't recognize. Fortunately, they didn't look as dusty as the rest of the items in the store.

After studying the various kinds, he settled on two gooey cashew-filled chocolate bars called Macaw Mud Pies and walked toward the counter.

He'd just rung a small bell, hoping to summon a cashier, when the sound of voices shouting outside grabbed his attention. Andy gazed through a nearby window and saw with disgust that it was none other than Bartlemore shouting at his assistant about being careful with the camera equipment he was carrying.

The Hollywood actor's shiny plane was parked nearby.

Andy rolled his eyes, ignoring the exchange, and turned back to the counter. Bartlemore seemed intent on following them no matter how hard they tried to get rid of him.

"Hello? Anybody here?" he called. Peering behind the counter, he saw an open door leading to a back room. Andy walked behind the cash register and peeked through the door. A light was on at the bottom of a worn staircase. He paused for a moment, unsure as to whether he should disturb the person below, but then called down.

"Excuse me!"

There was no answer.

"I'm just going to leave money on the counter," Andy called. "Two candy bars and a postcard."

Still no reply.

Andy shrugged and walked back to the counter. He took out his Zoomwriter and grabbed a scrap of paper from the receipt pad. Andy had just finished writing the note to let whoever was in charge know that he'd left the money for the items he'd purchased when he heard a sound that made him jump.

ROOOOAAAAR!

Andy whirled toward the window and saw, to his horror, that Yaw's plane was starting up.

They're leaving without me!

With his heart pounding nearly as fast as the propellers were turning, Andy rushed out the door and, waving his arms wildly, yelled for the plane to stop. He raced after the aircraft, hoping to get someone's attention before it took off.

"Hey! Wait! I'm still here! Stop!" he shouted.

But Andy was not loud enough to be heard over the roar of the engine. And although he ran as fast as he could, he could not catch up with the plane rolling resolutely down the wide swath of dirt.

The wind from the propellers nearly knocked Andy off his feet as, with a loud whine and a deafening roar, the airplane rose into the air, leaving him standing there with a shocked expression on his face.

"I can't believe they l-left without me," he stuttered. Andy gazed stupidly at the flashing running lights on the wings of Yaw's plane as the aircraft receded farther and farther from sight.

With a sickening feeling in the pit of his stomach, Andy wondered what he should do. But no sooner had he had the thought than a jovial and all-too-familiar voice spoke from somewhere behind him.

"Tough luck, son. Need a lift?"

Chapter Ten

The *Flying Phantom*

Andy sighed. He supposed he really didn't have any choice *but* to accept Bartlemore's offer. Well, technically he *did* have a choice, but hanging out in the middle of nowhere and hoping his companions would notice he was gone and then come back seemed somewhat foolish when he could more easily board Bartlemore's plane and catch up with them. As much as Andy didn't like him, going with the actor certainly seemed like the best choice.

Andy walked up the stairs and boarded the striking steel-plated plane. Once he was through the doorway, he couldn't help being impressed by the lavish surroundings.

"Welcome aboard the *Phantom*," Bartlemore said. "Have a seat."

The actor indicated a regal leather seat at a table with a linen tablecloth.

Andy sat down and Bartlemore took the seat opposite him. *This plane makes Yaw's look like a toy*, Andy thought. The walls were covered with a rich, polished mahogany, and all the fixtures had gold fittings. The window next to him had cream-colored curtains, and in a small holder next to his armrest was a neat arrangement of newspapers.

Andy noticed that Charlie the cameraman had taken a seat toward the back of the plane. He was without his camera for the first time.

A man in a crisp uniform and dark glasses who Andy assumed was the pilot leaned down next to Bartlemore and said something low in his ear. Bartlemore nodded, and the man walked up to the cockpit.

Andy studied Bartlemore. His expression had changed from the one that he'd presented to the group before. Gone was the smug smile and jovial devil-may-care attitude. In its place was a graver, more focused expression.

Neither of them spoke as the plane's engine started and the massive aircraft rolled down the runway in the same direction Yaw and the others had gone.

As they roared skyward, Bartlemore absorbed himself in reading something in a leatherbound folder. At first, Andy wondered if it might be a script—perhaps lines he was memorizing for a film. But try as he might, he couldn't get a glimpse of whatever it was Bartlemore was reading.

When the plane had leveled off, a woman in a flight uniform appeared with a silver teapot and two china cups. Placing them in front of Andy and Bartlemore, she asked, "Will you be having luncheon?"

Bartlemore glanced at Andy and then said, "I expect the boy's hungry. Do we have any sandwiches left in the galley?"

"I think so," she replied.

"Let's have those. Thanks, Virginia."

The woman smiled and nodded, then turned and walked back down the aisle.

Bartlemore leveled his gaze at Andy. The actor seemed to be studying him, as if weighing something in his mind. It took only a few moments of that unbreakable gaze for Andy to grow uncomfortable. He was about to ask Bartlemore what was bothering him when the actor's expression relaxed. Seeming to have made up his mind about something, Bartlemore broke the silence between them.

"I'm not exactly who you think I am, Andy Stanley. But I know all about you and can assure you that I mean you no harm."

Andy was taken aback. "What are you saying? That you're not John Bartlemore, the actor? Not to seem disrespectful, but I've seen you in plenty of films. Plus there's the fact that you've been following us around with that camera."

Bartlemore chuckled. "I am indeed John Bartlemore. But the whole *I'm out here on a movie shoot and happened to find you all by accident* thing is just an act. I'm a federal agent working for the US government."

Now it was Andy's turn to laugh. Bartlemore? A secret agent? It was too much to believe! "Sorry, but you must think I'm pretty naive if you expect me to believe that. No offense . . ."

Bartlemore waved the comment aside. "None taken. And I'm glad you're skeptical. It only proves that up to this point, everything has been going perfectly according to plan. But let me help allay your skepticism."

Bartlemore reached into his coat pocket and removed a small wallet. He flipped it open and handed it to Andy. At the sight of it, Andy's eyes nearly popped out of his head. It was a badge and an ID. And unless they were exceptionally good forgeries, everything about them seemed genuine.

"I . . . I didn't . . ."

Bartlemore replaced the wallet in his pocket with a toothy grin. "Hard to believe, but there it is. Tea?"

Andy nodded weakly. Bartlemore poured tea into each of their cups, and Andy, his hands shaking a little, took a sip from the excellent brew to steady his nerves.

"The reason I'm following you is because I am not only a close friend of your grandfather's, but I am also trying to prevent a major catastrophe."

"You know my grandfather?" Andy asked.

"Ned Lostmore? Of course. Known him for years. I was very sorry to hear about his unfortunate . . . change. Truth is, we warned him about exploring that temple in the first place. We expected an ambush from the Collective."

"You know about them, too?" Andy blurted.

"There's very little we don't know about the Jungle Explorers' Society and its enemies. Your grandfather keeps us abreast of all the artifacts under his protection. Once he made you his new Keymaster, we knew it would only be a matter of time before we met you."

Bartlemore looked troubled. "I'd hoped it wouldn't be under such unfortunate circumstances, but I've been waiting for a chance to pull you aside. The fact that you missed the plane with the others provided the perfect opportunity for us to talk."

The flight attendant returned with a silver tray piled high with delicious-looking sandwiches. Andy felt extremely hungry all of a sudden and was very happy for the distraction. He was having a hard time registering everything Bartlemore had told him. He bit into a sandwich of thickly sliced ham on fluffy white bread as he listened to the agent continue.

"You're aware that your grandfather has been concerned that there's a spy in your midst?"

Andy nodded as he chewed. Ned had told him as much at the end of his last adventure. Professor Phink had been a step ahead of them the entire time they'd been searching for the Pailina Pendant, and Ned was convinced that the Jungle Explorers' Society's whereabouts and intentions had been compromised by a traitor.

"We have a pretty good idea who it is," Bartlemore said. "But the last thing we need is for them to think that we're on to them. The camera Charlie is carrying isn't a camera at all, by the way. It's a weapon."

Andy boggled at him. "A weapon?"

Bartlemore nodded. "Why do you think we have it pointed at Rusty Bucketts all the time?"

Andy gasped. "You mean that he . . . Rusty . . . is the traitor? But that's impossible!"

Bartlemore sighed. "I know it's a lot to take in. But at this point, he's our most likely suspect. He's close to your grandfather and knows most of what the Society has planned before anyone else."

"But I can't believe that. We're friends! And besides, I've seen him fight. He battled Professor Phink's men with the rest of us. He can't be a spy!"

"We're not absolutely certain, but the evidence is

mounting against him. We think that he's working as a double agent."

Andy's mind reeled with the implications. Rusty was the de facto leader of the group when his grandfather wasn't around. The only person who held a higher rank was Abigail's father, Albert.

Bartlemore's gaze softened as he watched the conflicting emotions playing over Andy's face. "Look, son, I know it's difficult to accept. But if what we think is indeed true, then this particular mission could be one of the most hazardous the Society has ever undertaken. Your grandfather wanted you to be aware so that you could take extra precautions."

The special agent opened the leatherbound folder he'd been studying earlier and pushed it across the table to Andy. The boy gazed down at a black-and-white photo of an old painting. Examining it, Andy could see that it depicted an Incan warrior in a feathered head-dress, holding something aloft in his hand.

"What is it?" Andy asked.

"That is the Golden Paw. Or a painting of it, anyway. If our enemies get it before we do, the world as we know it could come to an end."

Andy squinted at the painting, trying to make out the details. He could see that the man holding the golden ornament was standing on a pile of bones and that he wore an exultant expression.

"I thought that my grandfather was going to let us know what was going on when we got to Cuzco. How do you know about this?"

"Your grandfather and I have already been in contact. What I'm about to tell you is nothing that you won't find out soon enough. But it's important that you know now so that you'll know what to do when we get there."

Andy listened as Bartlemore detailed what the legend said that the Golden Paw was capable of. As the agent spoke, Andy couldn't help wondering if he was off his rocker. Even though Andy had seen what magic could do on his last adventure, the Golden Paw's abilities seemed too fantastic to believe.

"So what you're saying is that not only can anyone who possesses it transform themselves to look like someone else, but that it also gives the wearer super-human strength?"

"So the legends say." Bartlemore looked thoughtful. "But, truth be told, nobody is quite sure how it works. In fact, as you know, until we received intelligence that the Collective was actively searching for it, we didn't even think that it was real."

"I can see why," Andy said thoughtfully. He closed the folder and passed it back to Bartlemore. "So if the Collective gets their hands on it first, they'll be able to impersonate anybody they want to. Then what? Steal money? Rob banks? Impersonate world leaders?" Andy asked.

Bartlemore nodded. "Probably. We don't know all their plans, but just think of the implications. All the world's secrets laid bare to a criminal mastermind. We just can't afford to let that happen."

"And you think Rusty is working for them? That

he'll steal the Golden Paw once we find it?"

"More than likely," Bartlemore said. "That's why we're going to stick close. We know that the Collective is searching for the paw, but we suspect they are hedging their bets in case we find it before they do. When you reunite with the others, Bucketts will probably make following you difficult for Charlie and me. I need you to leave some kind of bread-crumb trail for us to follow if he gets too tricky. Besides, you're going to want Charlie and me nearby should you get into trouble."

Andy looked uncomfortable as Bartlemore continued. "Look, there's a lot riding on this. If Bucketts gets his hands on the paw, what could be simpler than claiming that the Jungle Explorers' Society has beaten the Collective, only to turn the paw over to them shortly thereafter?"

"But why would he do that?" Andy asked. "He just doesn't seem like the type of guy who would betray his friends for personal gain."

Bartlemore's expression hardened. "People aren't

always what they appear to be. Look at me. Would you have expected a silly jungle serial actor to work for the government?"

Andy had to admit to himself that Bartlemore was right. It was certainly something he'd have never considered before.

Andy sighed and ran a hand through his hair. "Okay, so you said that you and my grandfather want me to be prepared. What is it you need me to do?"

Bartlemore leaned forward in his chair. "You're the Keymaster. If we actually *do* find the Golden Paw, we need you to lock it up in this. . . ."

Bartlemore reached under his seat and produced a sturdy-looking box with a small brass key. Andy gazed at it skeptically.

"What's to keep Rusty, or whoever the spy is, from just attacking me and grabbing the box? It doesn't seem very safe."

"Watch," Bartlemore said. He inserted the key into the box and lifted the lid. "When you get the Golden

Paw, you'll put it in here and then press this button."

Andy watched as Bartlemore pressed a small switch positioned underneath the lid. A loud humming noise filled the air, and Andy felt the little hairs on his arms stand on end. It was like some kind of powerful energy was emanating from the box.

The next thing Andy knew, the box began to shimmer and then, amazingly, it faded from view.

Andy couldn't believe his eyes! The strange humming noise stopped, and the energy field that he'd been experiencing faded with it.

"Where'd it go?" he said, awestruck.

"It's still here, only it's invisible," Bartlemore said with a grin. "Your grandfather lent us this. It's an artifact from the Middle Ages called the Ghost Box. He thought it might come in handy for this mission."

Bartlemore felt around what must have been the edge of the box and reinserted the tiny key. Once again, the strange noise filled the air, as did the tingling sensation. Then the box shimmered back into focus.

"Amazing," Andy said.

Bartlemore handed Andy the key and the box. "You're to keep both of these with you at all times. When we find the Golden Paw, I'll distract Bucketts with the fake camera. It'll be up to you to grab it and put it in the box without anyone seeing you do it. Then replace the paw with this. . . ."

He held up a replica of the artifact in the painting. It was a beautiful sculpture of a monkey's hand that appeared to Andy to have been created from real gold.

Andy took it from Bartlemore. Judging by its heavy weight, he could only assume that his suspicion had been correct.

"But how do you know if the painting is correct? What if the real Golden Paw looks different?"

Bartlemore waved off the question. "The main thing is to try to buy us time for you to hide the real one. Hopefully it looks close enough. If you can get your girlfriend to put it in a bag and hand it to Bucketts, he probably won't even think that it's been switched."

Andy blushed at the inference. "Abigail's not my girlfriend," he said.

"Sure, kid," Bartlemore said. And Andy noticed that just a bit of the smug expression he'd carried when playing the part of a pompous Hollywood actor had returned.

As Bartlemore settled back in his seat, Andy thought more about the plan. There were so many things that could go wrong. And he was still having a really hard time believing that his friend, whom he looked up to, could actually be a traitor.

Andy stared out the window at the darkness. *He didn't say it was for sure that Rusty is the traitor,* Andy thought. *Maybe he's got it all wrong.*

But if that were true, it raised an even more unsettling question. Could one of the others in the expedition be the traitor?

And if so, who?

Chapter Eleven
A Reunion of Sorts

When the plane landed, Andy was relieved to see his friends waiting for him. Evidently, the pilot on the *Flying Phantom* had not notified Yaw that they were coming, because he didn't see her in the group. Had she flown back to find him?

The landing strip was much more rustic than the one that they'd been on earlier. To Andy's eyes, it looked like little more than a grassy field. It was positioned next to a winding river, one that Andy assumed from his geography lessons was the Amazon.

A grass shack with no markings on it stood on stilts on the river's bank. Andy's friends gathered there, all eyes anxiously on Bartlemore's plane as it taxied to a stop.

None of them know who he really is, Andy thought. *They probably think I've spent the whole plane ride listening to him brag about his various accomplishments.*

Andy noticed Rusty's hardened expression as he gazed through the window. A light rain had started to fall, evidently adding to the bush pilot's sour mood. It was obvious to Andy that his discomfort at seeing Bartlemore's plane and having to interact with him once more was weighing on his mind.

Could he really be a traitor? Andy wondered. The thought made his stomach flip-flop. It would be so much easier to believe the best of one of his grandfather's closest allies. How in the world would Andy be able to keep acting like nothing was wrong around Rusty, all the while watching him closely to see if he would betray the group?

I wonder if I should tell Abigail what's going on, Andy thought. He knew that Bartlemore would be against it and that he might be compromising a government mission, but he didn't think he could keep the knowledge to himself. He needed someone he could trust. And, ironically, it was a person who until recently had worked for the very same enemy Rusty was now accused of colluding with.

If he thought about it, it was surprising that Bartlemore didn't suspect Abigail as the spy rather than Rusty. After all, wouldn't she have been the obvious choice?

But for whatever reason, that wasn't the case. And in Andy's opinion, it would be foolish to think that Abigail could possibly be a traitor. He'd gotten to know her well over the last few months and knew with absolute certainty that she wouldn't do it.

Now that she has a good relationship with her father again, she'd never want to jeopardize that.

The plane rolled to a stop and the big door swung open, the collapsible staircase extending to the ground. Bartlemore ushered Andy to the door and, with a conspiratorial wink, followed him down the stairs, waving broadly at the crowd and reverting once more to his alter ego.

"You'll want to thank me, of course," he boomed. "Dan Daring saves the day again! The boy is safe and completely unharmed!"

Andy was surprised when Abigail and Betty and Dotty rushed forward and embraced him in a group hug. Judging from the relief on their faces, they'd really been worried about him.

"Where were you?" Abigail exclaimed. "One minute you were there, and the next you were gone! When I first woke up, I thought you might have gone to the bathroom or something. Yaw stayed behind to look for you while Rusty flew us here. We couldn't afford to wait any longer. Not if we want to beat the Collective to the paw. . . ."

She looked simultaneously angry and upset, and Andy felt even more terrible about missing the plane. He'd had no idea that his absence would cause such anxiety.

"I'm sorry. I thought I'd run over to the shop for a second, just to stretch my legs. I guess the time got away from me," he confessed. "Is Yaw on her way here now?"

Abigail shrugged. "We haven't heard from her. For all we know, she's still looking for you."

"Next time you're planning on running off, wake one of us up first," Betty said.

Dotty nodded, her lips pursed in a thin line. "The mission is dangerous enough as it is."

"Understood," Andy said meekly. Then, remembering why he'd left the plane in the first place, he reached his hand into his pocket and pulled out the candy bar he'd bought for Abigail.

"I guess it's pretty stupid now," he said, offering it to her. "But at the time, I thought you might be hungry."

Abigail took it and smiled. Then she hit him lightly

on the shoulder. "It was stupid to risk being abandoned in the jungle for chocolate. But since you're back and you're okay . . ."

She peeled off the wrapper and took a bite of the gooey bar, then rolled her eyes in pleasure.

"Mmm. Maybe it *was* worth it after all."

Andy chuckled. Behind him, Rusty stepped forward, looking awkward. He cleared his throat and offered his meaty hand to Andy. Andy shook it. Gazing up at the big man's face, Andy got the impression that Rusty was not only glad to see him, but that he'd been worried about him as well.

"Don't ever do that again, understand?"

Andy nodded. "Yes, sir."

Rusty seemed satisfied with his response and grunted his approval.

Suddenly, Andy felt a hand on his shoulder. He turned and nearly jumped at the monstrous face staring back at him. Then Andy realized he wasn't looking at a face, but at a fearsome tribal mask.

"Cedric!"

"Andy! Great to see you, lad! It's been a while, what?"

The Cambridge-educated witch doctor wore an incongruous blue suit in addition to the mask, looking to Andy like a wealthy businessman on his way to a Halloween party.

Cedric noticed Andy looking at his suit and said, "A bit of tricky business at a nearby village. The chief had a terrible case of the Amazonian Squints. He could barely see, and insisted that everyone wear their Sunday best out of respect. Obviously, I was the only one there in a suit. The rest of them had, ah, rather *interesting* ideas about what *Sunday best* meant. Anyway, after I gave him the cure, I forgot to change."

"But why did he care what everyone looked like if he couldn't see?" Andy asked. "It doesn't make sense."

Cedric ignored the question, focusing instead on Bartlemore.

"Are you indeed the actor John Bartlemore?" he exclaimed.

"I am indeed," said Bartlemore with a smug grin. "Care for an autograph, my friend?"

"Would I care for . . . *of course!*" Cedric shouted happily. "I've seen every one of your films at least ten times! You're magnificent, Mr. Bartlemore. Simply magnificent! My wife, Margaret, agrees."

He's married? Andy thought. *Wow. That's a surprise!*

Because nobody had ever seen Cedric when he wasn't wearing a mask, it was hard to imagine him leading a normal life. Andy wondered if his wife wore a mask, too. He snickered at thought of the entire Bunsen family, kids included, all gathered around the dinner table with elaborate tribal masks on.

Abigail looked at him quizzically, and Andy shook his head. "I'll tell you later," he whispered. "Just had a funny thought, that's all."

Abigail nodded and continued nibbling at her candy bar. Andy noticed that Bartlemore and Rusty were avoiding each other as much as possible, but the tension in the air between them was palpable. It was broken by Cedric.

"By Jove, let's get cracking. Ned sent me a communiqué, and I have some clues to the temple where the Golden Paw is rumored to be hidden."

"Right you are," Rusty said. He turned to Bartlemore. "We'll be discussing our plans in private. Should you choose to follow us from this point forward, it will be at your own peril."

Bartlemore seemed unfazed by the comment. He just smiled, nodded, and motioned for Charlie to keep "filming." Now that Andy knew the camera Charlie held was fake, it made him nervous to see it pointed at Rusty.

Bartlemore never said exactly what kind of weapon it was. I wonder what it does.

Rusty motioned for the group to join him in the nearby shack. Andy was the last one to go inside, and when he glanced back at Bartlemore, the man gave him a slight nod.

Andy returned it. He knew what he was supposed to do, but he was having a hard time not feeling torn in two by Bartlemore's proposal. It made him sick to think that the people he'd trusted with his life might also be traitors.

I wish my grandfather were here, Andy thought. *He'd know what to do.*

A sudden thought made Andy halt in his tracks. The Zoomwriter had the ability to send wireless messages! He could telegraph his grandfather when he put the pen into transmission mode!

Feeling a surge of relief, Andy reached into his coat pocket for his pen. His eyes widened as he patted desperately at the pocket. It was empty!

Where is it? He removed his jacket and probed every possible hiding place. After a few moments of searching, he realized with a terrible, sinking feeling what had happened. He'd left his pen on the counter at Trader Sam's. He'd been in such a hurry to catch the plane, he'd left his most precious possession behind.

Andy's face paled. As he took his seat with the others in the abandoned shack, he felt like crying. *How could I have been so stupid?*

Rusty began giving details of the mission, but Andy barely heard him. His mind was spinning. All he could think about was the pen—the only gift his grandfather had ever given him—and how priceless it was. Now he might never see it again. This was his big second chance to prove himself, and he was blowing it!

Andy felt sick to his stomach as Cedric took over the meeting and outlined the dangerous route that they would have to travel to the location of the Golden Paw. His odds of surviving the mission and coming out on top seemed to be at an all-time low.

Chapter Twelve

A Message
from Yaw

The next morning, the group was delighted to find a carrier pigeon from the Jungle Air Mail service waiting with a message from Yaw. Rusty had discovered it when packing their gear for the first leg of the journey to the Temple of the Golden Paw and had happily shared the news with the others.

Andy Stanley spotted with Bartlemore by local shopkeeper. Flying back to HQ to refuel. Awaiting further instructions.

Y.R.

"Good ol' Yaw!" Rusty exclaimed. "She's just fine. I'll let her know we have the boy."

Andy bristled at the word *boy*. He was twelve! He wasn't a kid who needed to be babysat by the others! Andy glanced at Abigail to see if she'd noticed the slight, but it didn't appear she had. Even so, Andy made a vow to himself to do what it took to improve his standing with the group. He'd show them that he was one of them, not just some kid tagging along on their mission.

Suddenly, a thought entered Andy's mind that he hadn't considered before. If what Bartlemore said was true and Rusty was a spy, was it possible that he was trying to get under Andy's skin? What if Rusty was deliberately trying to get Andy to quit the mission? Rusty knew that Andy was Ned Lostmore's grandson and that he would report everything to him.

Was it possible? Rusty hadn't seemed too eager to have him along on the mission. In fact, he had only agreed because Ned had ordered him to. Rusty had looked concerned when Andy showed up with Bartlemore. At the time, Andy had assumed Rusty was just concerned for his safety, but what if the real concern was that Bartlemore and Andy had found them?

As Andy helped the others load their gear, he resolved to keep a close eye on Rusty. The more he thought about the bush pilot, the more suspicious he grew.

This "boy" is a lot smarter than they realize, Andy thought, and he was comforted by the idea as he helped Cedric lift a particularly heavy pack onto one of the mules they would be taking into the jungle.

When everything was loaded up, Rusty called out, "We walk from here." Then he added a comment directed at Bartlemore, who was also up and ready to follow them. "I'm warning you for your own good,

Bartlemore. We'll be following a treacherous path. For your own safety, you should take that plane of yours and fly back to Hollywood."

Bartlemore flashed him a large grin and waved. "We've come too far to go back now, but thank you for considering our well-being."

Andy noticed that Bartlemore's grin faded when Rusty turned around. The actor nodded at Andy and gave him a knowing stare, as if to say *Remember what we talked about.*

The group set off at a brisk pace, heading from the edge of the Amazon into a thicket of trees and heavy undergrowth. Andy, who had been given the task of leading one of the two mules that had been left for their use at the hut, soon found that his charge was particularly stubborn and not at all interested in the idea of going into such difficult terrain.

"Come on, girl," Andy coaxed. "Will . . . you . . . just . . . *please* . . . stop fighting?" Andy tugged on the rope, trying to force the mule down the muddy trail, but the mule barely inched forward, evidently more frustrated than soothed by Andy's efforts. Abigail, who was ahead with the others, noticed that Andy was lagging behind and came back to see what was wrong.

"She'll only get more stubborn the harder you pull," she advised. Andy's face was beet red from effort, and sweat stood out on his forehead.

"Fine, you give it a try," he said, flipping the reins to Abigail. The girl moved close to the mule and began whispering soothingly into its rabbitlike ears. The whites around the mule's eyes slowly vanished. Petting the mule's head, Abigail reached into her pocket and pulled out a small piece of dried fruit. She handed it to the eager animal, which happily began to trot forward.

"Well, that was pretty impressive," Andy said.

"My dad had horses when I was little. I learned that patience is pretty important when trying to get them to do anything."

Andy, Abigail, and the mule walked on. They were

quite a bit behind the others, but they found that the trail Rusty had blazed was easy to follow.

Andy swatted a mosquito that had landed on his neck. The deeper they went into the humid jungle, the more the bugs seemed to thrive. As annoying as the insects were, they were nothing compared to the nagging suspicions about Rusty that were growing in Andy's mind.

Andy glanced over at Abigail. He wondered if it was okay to share with her what Bartlemore had told him. Abigail seemed to be lost in thoughts of her own. Andy couldn't help noticing just how pretty she was. The dappled sunlight played on her cheeks, and her hair was up in a loose bun. Abigail never wore jewelry, and she wasn't a fancy dresser, but there was something about her spirit, her determination and conviction, that Andy admired.

"What?" Abigail asked suddenly.

"What, what?" Andy replied.

"You were staring," Abigail said.

"Oh, uh . . . sorry," said Andy. "I was just thinking."

"Thinking about what?"

Andy bit his lip. Bartlemore worked for the government, and he had told Andy about Rusty in confidence. Would Andy get in trouble for talking? But the more he wrestled with his secret, the more he couldn't resist the comfort that would come from sharing it with someone. And, glancing around, he saw that there was no one else in earshot. He decided to try a subtle approach.

"How long have you known Rusty?" Andy asked.

Abigail glanced at him. "Rusty and my father met during the war. They served in the same battalion. Rusty actually fought the Red Baron, did you know that? My father was an airline mechanic back then, and he helped keep Rusty's plane in the air."

"Wow," Andy said. "Has Rusty ever told you about it?"

"Not really," Abigail said. "He tends to keep a lot to himself. I guess he lost a lot of friends in the war and doesn't like to talk about it. My father told me that

Rusty was an ace who shot down over thirty planes."

Andy's mind swirled. How could a military veteran with such an impressive record be working as a spy for criminals? It just didn't make sense.

"Why do you ask?" Abigail asked. "You've been acting strange ever since you came back with Bartlemore. Are you sure everything's okay?"

It was an opening Andy couldn't resist. After breathing a heavy sigh, he said, "When I was with Bartlemore, he told me that he's a special agent for the government and Rusty is a spy for the Collective."

It all came out in a rush. Abigail's eyes widened at the news, and then, to Andy's surprise, she burst out laughing.

"You're kidding! Rusty a spy? Bartlemore a government agent? And you believed him?"

Andy felt his cheeks redden. "He was pretty convincing. He showed me his badge and everything."

Abigail's smile faded. "You're not joking. Okay. Well, first of all, Rusty is the Jungle Explorers' Society's most loyal member. What about all the things he did in the last mission? Remember?"

Andy's expression was troubled. "Of course I do. But...but what if all of that was an act? What if he's secretly working with the Collective, and what Bartlemore says is true? My grandfather said that there was a spy leaking information to them. How would Bartlemore know that unless he'd talked to Ned himself?"

Abigail was quiet for a few moments before replying. The only sound among them was the sucking sound the mule's hooves made in the wet earth and the distant sound of branches snapping and insects buzzing. Andy was starting to grow worried that he'd offended her somehow when she replied, "If there's anybody I don't trust at this point, it's Bartlemore. How he knows so much about us and found us so conveniently back at our camp is suspicious in and of itself. I'm actually surprised that he doesn't think *I'm* the spy. I would be the most likely candidate, considering the fact that I worked with Professor Phink and the Collective before."

Andy nodded. He felt a little better now that Abigail had pointed out Rusty's stellar record of loyalty. "You're probably right about Rusty. And by the way, Bartlemore isn't one hundred percent convinced that Rusty is the spy. He seems suspicious of everyone. Maybe we should be more suspicious about him."

"That's what I think," said Abigail.

But in spite of her feelings on the matter, Andy couldn't help thinking about how official Bartlemore's credentials had looked and how convincing he'd been. He was ashamed of himself for letting Bartlemore sow seeds of doubt about his friends, but he couldn't shake the thought that there was a possibility the actor turned agent might be right.

Andy was miserable. His head was full of suspicions that he could not confirm or deny. But he supposed there wasn't much he could do now either way. So, plodding along beside the mule, he tried to pass the time by making light conversation with Abigail.

Finally, after what felt like several hours, they caught

up with the others. They had come to a dead stop at a clearing in the brush.

When Andy saw what lay in front of them, all thoughts about spies and loyalty and betrayal fled his mind, and a sudden rush of terrible, crippling dread washed over him.

Chapter Thirteen
The Death Maze

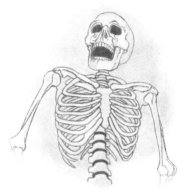

The gigantic skeleton was about thirty feet tall. Its jaws were open and its teeth were bared in a hungry, vicious smile. Fortunately, it was made of stone. But the mere sight of such a forbidding statue made Andy's knees turn to water.

This can't be good.

"Well, my friends, it looks like we've arrived at the location mentioned in the ancient manuscript Cedric discovered. Want to take it from here, Ced?" said Rusty.

Cedric, now clothed in a safari outfit and wearing his usual tribal mask, nodded. "Righto! The manuscript Ned and I discovered was hidden in a tomb that once held an important artifact—the Spear of Quetzalcoatl. We retrieved the spear long ago, but it wasn't until recently that we thought to look inside the shaft of the spear itself for clues. It turned out to be hollow, and contained clues to the Golden Paw. According to the legend on the manuscript, the great king Quetzal-Ra was so worried about someone finding the Golden Paw that he created an elaborate security system to protect it. If what I've read is true, only he knew how to safely navigate the obstacles that would keep thieves away from the temple in which it's hidden.

"The tunnel in front of us is supposed to lead to the temple. Its name can be roughly translated as the 'Death Maze.' There are few records of people trying to navigate it, as almost none lived to tell the tale. Very few explorers that have gone inside have ever returned, and some say that the maze itself is haunted with their spirits."

He glanced up at the huge skeleton. "The statue placed in front of the cave entrance shows us that we've found the right location. It's meant to serve as a warning not to proceed."

Bartlemore, who had been walking behind the group, stepped forward, beaming his usual annoying smile. "Make sure you get all this, Charlie. Keep rolling!" he said over his shoulder. "We're going to make a million on this, mark my words."

Rusty scowled at Bartlemore. It was a look of such loathing and hatred that it seemed to Andy that, had it been able to, Rusty's gaze would have killed Bartlemore on the spot.

Charlie gave Bartlemore a thumbs-up and kept turning the crank on the side of his camera, as if he were advancing the film inside. "Got it, J.B."

Andy couldn't help feeling uneasy as he watched Charlie point the camera at Rusty. Knowing that there wasn't any film inside, but rather a dangerous weapon, made him look at the entire situation differently. The conflicting emotions about whether or not he should tell Rusty about its being a weapon rose again. His indecision, coupled with discomfort at the giant skeleton rising in front of him, made his stomach lurch.

"Are you all right?" Abigail asked with a worried expression. "You look really pale."

"I'm fine," Andy managed.

But he didn't feel that way.

Cedric continued with his speech. "If one can navigate the three gateways inside, the temple is supposedly at the center of the maze. And if the intelligence gathered by Ned is correct, then we haven't much time before our enemies are upon us, so we'd better get cracking."

"How do we know that those scalawags are behind us?" demanded Rusty. "They could already be inside for all we know!"

"Ah, but we can tell," Cedric said proudly. "Follow me over here, if you please."

The thin Englishman led them to a cave opening

not far from the statue. Above the rough-hewn entry was a stone lintel carved with ancient symbols. Andy studied the creepy images of skulls, bones, and some kind of demonic thing with fangs. He tried to swallow but found, without surprise, that his throat was dry.

Cedric pointed at a stone with the impression of a human hand on it to the left of the entrance. Upon closer inspection, Andy saw a small hole at the tip of the pointer finger.

"Entering the maze requires a blood offering. According to my research, this small hole actually conceals a needle. Anyone who wishes to go in must put their hand here and allow their finger to be pricked. The few accounts we have say that once the blood drips down to the base of the palm, the door opens."

For emphasis, Cedric knocked on the stone wall just behind the entryway. It sounded as solid as it looked.

"Since there's no fresh blood on the stone, I believe that we can safely assume that we've beaten the Collective here. Now then, who wants to go first?"

Andy definitely didn't. He tried to look as inconspicuous as possible as everyone exchanged nervous glances.

After a long moment, Rusty cleared his throat and, with a loud grunt, pushed Cedric out of the way. The beefy man slapped his hand down on the stone. "Do your worst!" he exclaimed.

They all held their breath. After a moment, Rusty let out a bark of surprise as something pierced the skin of his pointer finger. Seconds later, a trickle of blood flowed down the finger of the hand to the bottom of the palm impression.

At first, nothing happened. And then, with a mighty groan, the heavy stone wall began to roll backward into a hidden recess. Andy watched, openmouthed, as the door moved away. He was amazed at the skill of the ancients—that they had been capable of creating such a thing. How did it work? Was it the moisture of the blood?

It's ancient technology, Andy thought. *I'm sure that there's a simple scientific explanation for it.*

In spite of all he had seen, Andy clung to the notion of scientific explanation. The truth was, the scarier implication that the door was moved by something supernatural was something he didn't want to consider. He'd had a gnawing unease with the supernatural ever since his last adventure. Hawaiian gods were supposed to be myths. But what he'd witnessed had defied all logic.

Andy watched as Rusty slipped through the door, which slammed shut behind him. He'd hoped that entry would require only one blood offering—that they could all follow Rusty through—but that didn't seem to be the case. *Of course not,* he thought bitterly. *That would be too easy.*

One by one, Andy's friends opened the door and entered the maze. Soon, only he, Bartlemore, and the cameraman were left. Andy tried his best to keep his hand from shaking. He was about to set his palm on the indentation when Bartlemore grabbed his shoulder and whispered, "Remember, no matter what happens, don't let Rusty Bucketts out of your sight. If we get separated, leave some kind of sign or mark, and I'll try to catch up with you."

Andy nodded. Bartlemore, noticing his uneasy expression, gave him a slap on the back and assured him that there was nothing to fear.

But Andy wasn't so sure. He watched as his own blood dripped down the stone and the door slid open. Staring into the opening where the others had walked into the darkness beyond, he murmured, "Here goes nothing." And then, his heart hammering in his chest, he crossed over the threshold and heard the heavy stone door slam shut behind him.

Chapter Fourteen
A Surprising Departure

It took a few moments for Andy's eyes to adjust to the darkness. For a panicky second or two, it felt like he was wearing a blindfold, and he worried that he wouldn't be able to see a thing! But after a minute or so, he found that he could make out some very dim shadows in front of him. He reached out a hand to steady himself as he walked forward, but immediately recoiled as his hand brushed the wall. It was covered with some kind of slime!

"Careful there, son," came Rusty's familiar voice. "Those walls are covered with something foul."

"I noticed," Andy replied, wiping his hand on his trousers. He automatically sniffed his fingers to see if they were clean and nearly gagged at the stench.

Rusty chuckled from somewhere nearby. "I'm not sure, but it might be bat guano," the big man said. Andy felt Rusty grip his shoulder and push him gently forward. "This way. Cedric is trying to get some torches lit, and I'm sure we can spare a little water so that you can wash up."

Andy was eager to wash. The very idea that there were bats somewhere above gave him the willies, not to mention the idea that they'd been there so long they'd coated the walls with their droppings.

Suddenly, there was a bright flash of light. Andy, who had grown accustomed to the darkness, shielded his eyes against the blinding glare. When he was able to focus again, he was relieved to see Cedric standing nearby with a flaming torch in his hand.

His relief was temporary. There was a sudden rush of flapping wings and high-pitched shrieks as hundreds of bats, all startled by the sudden light, came flying past the top of his head.

"AIEEEEE!" Andy screamed. He would have been mortified about how high-pitched his voice sounded, but he couldn't help it. The beating wings were all around him, and he swung wildly at the air, trying to swat the beasts away.

As quickly as they'd come, the bats were gone. As Andy stood there, wide-eyed and quivering, he was relieved to see that the others, especially Abigail, had been startled as well.

"They must have another way out," Cedric speculated. "There's no way around that door."

"That's good news," Rusty said. "It means that if we get trapped in here, we're sure to have fresh air."

True to his word, Rusty offered Andy a canteen and

a bar of soap. Andy quickly washed his hands and dried them on a small towel that Abigail had brought in her pack.

Now that there was light, everyone took the opportunity to look around and examine the tunnel. The walls that surrounded them were rough-hewn, but incredibly high. So high, in fact, the torchlight couldn't reach the ceiling the bats had flown down from.

The walls were well illuminated, though. Andy noticed the horrible slime dripping down from unseen heights and felt a wave of nausea.

"Here, have a peppermint," Abigail said. Andy accepted the candy gratefully and popped it in his mouth. He immediately felt relieved as the familiar cool mint flavor coated his mouth and brought comfort in the ominous surroundings.

"Let's move forward with extreme caution," Rusty said. "Be on the lookout for traps, and if you see anything suspicious at all, give a shout."

Andy shouldered his pack and followed the others,

keeping his eyes trained on Cedric, who was in the front next to Rusty, his torch raised against the gloomy darkness. The air had a damp, tomblike quality, and their footsteps echoed as they walked. There was also another smell, something dark and sinister that Andy couldn't place. Something like a mountain of moldy socks that lingered in the background.

Andy made a mental note to breathe as little as possible as he continued doggedly forward, trying his best not to get spooked. The candy helped his throat not feel too dry, but he was sucking it like crazy in an effort to calm himself down.

They hadn't proceeded more than twenty feet when Cedric let out a cry.

"AAAAAAAAAGH!"

At the sound of the scream, the entire tunnel was plunged back into darkness and there was a moment of terrible confusion and panic. Andy nearly crashed into Betty and Dotty.

"Blast it, where are the matches?" Rusty shouted.

"I've got some!" Abigail said.

There was the sound of some fumbling and then, a second later, a new torch was lit. But being able to see didn't make Andy feel any better. Just in front of them was a gaping hole. It had been covered with some kind of sticks or hay meant to make it blend in with the rocky floor. It seemed Cedric had walked right into it!

Rusty kneeled by the edge of the pit and shouted down into the darkness. "Cedric! Are you all right?"

There was no reply. Rusty lowered his torch as far down as he could, trying to see to the bottom of the pit, but the hole was evidently very, very deep. In spite of Rusty's torch, the bottom was swallowed in darkness, and there was not even the flicker of light from Cedric's torch below.

"Is he . . . ?" Andy started. But he knew the answer before he even finished his sentence. There was no possible way anyone could survive such a fall.

The group lowered their heads. Even Bartlemore, whom Andy hadn't noticed before, seemed at a loss for words. Betty and Dotty went over to Rusty and, in a very rare show of affection, wrapped their arms around him. Rusty looked overcome by grief.

Andy thought back to when he'd first met the highly educated man at his grandfather's funeral. Cedric had been really friendly and had even gifted Andy with a jar of crocodile teeth, a cure for some mysterious malady only he seemed to know.

He'd been a good man, and even though Andy hadn't known him very well, he immediately felt the loss. It seemed impossible to believe that one minute Cedric had been there, and the next he hadn't. It had happened so fast!

Andy glanced over at Abigail and noticed how shaken she looked. He wished he had something to give her, like the comforting peppermint that she'd offered him, but he didn't have anything. Instead, he moved closer to her and, after taking a deep breath, reached over and held her hand. Abigail looked startled at first. But she returned his gentle grip with a thankful squeeze.

They stood that way for a few minutes before Rusty announced in a hoarse voice that it was time to move forward. As a precaution, he suggested that everyone feel ahead in the darkness with anything they could find to test for traps. The conjoined twins tapped lightly with their katanas. Rusty had a hiking stick and waved it cautiously over the pathway ahead, scraping it gently on the floor. Because Andy and Abigail were in the middle of the pack, they weren't as vulnerable. But just to be safe, Andy took out a rope from his bag. He offered one end to Abigail and tied the other around his waist.

"That way if one of us falls, the other has a chance to save them," he said.

Abigail agreed and tied the end around her own waist.

The group moved even more cautiously now that they'd seen what terrible traps were in store for them. And if the going was slow, Andy didn't mind too much. The phrase "better safe than sorry" had more meaning to him than ever now.

The tunnel twisted and turned, and several times the group was forced to choose between passages. Along the way they discovered three more of the hidden pits. Thankfully, due to their constant vigilance, nobody fell in. But each time they found one, they were all reminded of poor Cedric, and it cast a gloom over the expedition.

To Andy, it seemed like no matter which path they chose, they continued to head steadily downward. The lower they went, the closer and clammier the air grew. Andy shivered and zipped up the front of his leather flight jacket. As he continued to walk, he couldn't keep the images of giant cobwebs out of his mind. The downward slope felt like a spiral that was drawing him closer and closer to something monstrous, like a spider lurking in the center of its lair.

After about two hours of walking, Rusty called for a halt. Andy was relieved to slip off the straps of his pack and give his aching shoulders a break. After untying the rope that he and Abigail shared, he slumped to the ground. As Andy sat down, he glanced behind him and noticed that Bartlemore and his cameraman were no longer with them. "Has anyone seen Bartlemore?" he asked.

The others turned to him with surprised expressions. They'd been so intent on watching out for pitfalls, nobody had even noticed that he wasn't following them.

"He probably got lost in one of the side tunnels," Rusty grunted. "Good riddance, I say."

But Andy didn't know how to feel about his disappearance. What if he'd fallen down a pit, like Cedric? He couldn't remember exactly when he'd stopped hearing the sound of Charlie's camera crank and Bartlemore's footsteps.

He told me to leave him a trail marker, Andy thought. But now that it had come to it, he didn't know whether he should. Rusty had seemed truly upset over Cedric's disappearance. Would a traitor to the Jungle Explorers' Society have felt that way? What if Bartlemore was wrong and the traitor was somebody else?

Andy wished he had his Zoomwriter pen. He could

have used the wireless communication setting to send a telegraph to his grandfather and let him know that he needed help! He felt a renewed sense of loss at having left the valuable pen behind and smacked the side of his leg in frustration.

Abigail noticed and asked, "Something wrong?"

"I wish I still had my pen," Andy replied miserably.

Abigail looked surprised. "You lost it?"

Andy nodded. "Back at the place we landed, where I missed the plane. I left it on the counter in the store."

Abigail gave him a sympathetic look. "I'm sorry, Andy. I know how much that pen meant to you."

Andy's eyes burned, but he forced himself not to cry. "It's just that Bartlemore's missing and I don't know what to do. Remember what I told you? About you-know-who being a spy?"

Andy gestured at Rusty with a tilt of his head.

Abigail shrugged and whispered, "I still say that Bartlemore was off his rocker about all that. Besides, he might just be lost in a nearby tunnel. It's really a blessing in disguise. Ned wouldn't want him to film us finding the Golden Paw."

"Yeah, but what if he's hurt somewhere? We can't just not look for him," Andy said.

Abigail looked worried. "I don't want anybody to get hurt, either. Not even Bartlemore. But I don't think that Rusty will want us to go back and look for him. He could be anywhere! The fact that we've made it this far without dying is a big enough deal. Why would he risk our lives for someone he can't stand?"

Andy stood and brushed off his trousers.

"Where are you going?" Abigail asked.

Andy gave her a level stare. "To tell Rusty everything."

Chapter Fifteen
Full Disclosure

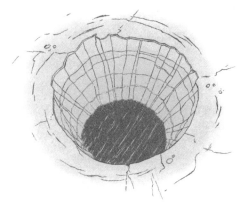

"He's a *what*?" roared Rusty.

"A government agent working with my grandfather. He said that you were a spy working for the Collective," Andy said sheepishly.

"And you *believed* him?" Rusty said. "Tell me that you didn't."

"Well . . . I . . ." Andy said. He fidgeted nervously. Now that he'd brought it out into the open, the charge that Rusty was a spy seemed ridiculous. The way Rusty looked at him with his big orange handlebar mustache twitching, Andy couldn't tell if he was about to laugh or rage at him.

It seemed like Rusty didn't know, either, and he started making a strangled choking sound that was somewhere between a guffaw and a shout.

"I've known your grandfather for years, boy, remember that. I swore an oath, and if you knew me half as well as he does, you would know that Rusty Bucketts is always true to his word. Bartlemore . . . that lowlife, sneaky, lying son of a . . ."

Betty shot Rusty a warning glance, and the big man stopped talking. Instead, his face red and flushed, Rusty took a moment to gather himself and gave Andy a serious stare.

"That two-bit excuse for an actor is no government agent, and—" he began.

"But he showed me his badge and ID," interrupted Andy.

Rusty held up his big hand to stop Andy short.

"Faking a badge and ID is easy enough to do, boy. Why, if you could see the phonies I've dealt with over the years, your hair would curl—"

But Rusty was suddenly interrupted by a long, keening wail. It was very loud and seemed to emanate from the darkness ahead of them. It sounded to Andy like a woman's voice, or some kind of tortured cat, and it made all the hairs on his arms stand on end.

"What was that?" Abigail asked.

"Shhh!" Betty and Dotty said in unison. In one fluid motion, the sisters grabbed fistfuls of throwing stars from the silken pouches at their waists.

The scorching red had drained from Rusty's face at the sound. It seemed as if the sound had affected him much the same way it had Andy. The big pilot reached into his rucksack and pulled out his slingshot. "Stand back Andy, Abigail," he hissed. "Betty and Dotty, you ladies are with me."

"Roger," Dotty said. Betty nodded in curt agreement with her sister.

A second wail, this one decidedly closer, echoed through the tunnel. Andy wheeled around to look behind him.

"It sounded like it came from over there," he said, pointing to the tunnel they'd come from.

"Time to move. Go, GO!" Rusty said.

The group rushed back down the passageway. As they all lurched forward, Andy suddenly had a thought.

"Wait, who's checking for—"

He'd been about to say the word *traps*, but just as it was about to leave his lips, another pair of screams, these ones all too human, sounded directly in front of him. Andy had barely enough time to see the heads of Betty and Dotty disappearing into a hidden pit when, without thinking, he leapt forward and grabbed the first thing his hand touched.

It turned out to be the scabbard of the katana Betty wore on her back. Before he knew it, Andy was sliding forward on his stomach, unable to bear the weight of two adults as they fell.

"Help!" he screamed. He was sliding headfirst after the twins when he felt Rusty's meaty grip on his heel.

"Got you!" Rusty shouted.

Andy gazed below and saw the panicked faces of Betty and Dotty staring up at him. His hand was wrapped around the cord that held the scabbard to the twins' backs, but the strain was too much. He could feel his grip slipping!

"I . . . I can't hold . . ."

And then, like a living nightmare, it happened. The cord snapped, and for a fleeting moment all he saw were the wide, horrified eyes of the sisters as they fell.

As with Cedric, it was over in a second. Andy stared down into the darkness with a feeling like descending an elevator shaft. He'd failed! Betty and Dotty were gone and it was his fault, because he hadn't been able to save them.

The world spun around him, everything shrinking to the size of a pinpoint. The words *My fault, all my fault* repeated over and over in his head.

He was dimly aware of more shrieking wails around him. As he lost consciousness, the ghostly cries mingled with the screams of Betty and Dotty as they fell down into the bottomless pit.

Then everything went black.

Chapter Sixteen
The Ghosts

Andy regained consciousness some time later. He didn't know how much time had passed, but he sensed one thing: he was completely alone. And, worse still, he was in total darkness.

"Hello?" he said softly. "Abigail? Anybody?"

There was no answer. Then the memory of what had happened to Betty and Dotty came back to him, and he felt a jolt of fear. Andy felt around in the dark for the edge of the pit into which they had fallen. Sure enough, his fingers brushed up against the drop-off.

They left me here, Andy thought. Then, with growing alarm, *They either left me or something got them. Maybe whatever was making those shrieks!*

Andy trembled uncontrollably as the thought took hold. What if they were all dead and he alone had survived? How could he possibly get out? Would he be stuck in the maze forever, and die either from starvation or by falling down into one of those hidden pits?

Sitting up, Andy slowly edged his way over to the wall. Thankfully, the surface wasn't covered with bat droppings, but the cold stone chilled him and did little to help stop his shaking.

His grandfather's word about a member of the Jungle Explorers' Society never leaving anyone behind came back to him, and Andy knew with mounting certainty that Rusty would have never done such a thing. His doubts about the stalwart bush pilot had vanished after he'd told him about the conversation with Bartlemore. And as for Abigail? Andy knew with certainty that she would have felt exactly the same.

That left only one conclusion. The only way that they would have left Andy behind was if something had gone terribly wrong. They must have been attacked by something in the darkness. But what did that mean for Andy? Should he try to navigate back up the path to where they had started? Poor Cedric had mentioned that the bats must have a way out. Perhaps that direction led to freedom.

"No. I'm g-going to f-find them," Andy said, his teeth chattering. "A Jungle Explorers' Society member doesn't l-leave anyone behind."

And as scared as he sounded to himself, he knew it was the right thing to do. He would try to rescue his friends. And if Rusty had been leading them downward into the tunnel rather than up, it seemed like that was the logical place to start.

Andy hadn't thought to bring a flashlight, which meant he was faced with the daunting challenge of edging his way along the wall in total darkness. He probed with his foot for any weakness on the trail ahead, hoping he would be able to anticipate any traps.

As he inched along, time seemed nonexistent. The only sounds were his breathing and shuffling steps as he went doggedly forward, aware of nothing but the next safe foothold.

It felt to him like several hours had passed when he finally rounded a corner of the cave wall and saw a tiny light in the distance. He'd been fortunate not to fall into any traps along the way and sagged with relief at being able to see anything at all.

Moving carefully, he approached the light source with furtive steps, still watching where he was going.

When he finally got there, he felt a mix of relief and horror. The relief came at seeing Abigail. But the horror came when he saw what had trapped her.

Andy didn't know how to describe the beings that floated in front of Abigail other than as three transparent apparitions. The first spirit was dressed like an

Incan god. He wore a feathered headdress and held a cruel-looking club. The second was a woman with long silver hair. Her face was a twisted mass of scars, and she stared at her captive with empty holes where her eyes should have been. The last—and worst, in Andy's opinion—was a skeletal thing that still had mummified skin hanging in tatters from its bones. The shrieks seemed to be coming from its hanging broken jaw as it hovered over the frightened girl.

As Andy took in the tears running down Abigail's face, the paralyzing fear he'd felt at seeing the apparitions melted away and was replaced with anger. The next thing he knew, Andy was running full bore at the hovering creatures, shouting at the top of his lungs, "Hey! Leave her alone!"

The apparitions turned. When the skeleton saw him, it let out another shriek and began floating in his direction. Andy didn't hesitate. He leapt in the direction of the ghosts, grabbing the rope he'd used to tie himself to Abigail and swinging it wildly above his head.

It was the only thing he had handy since he was without his pen, but it was better than nothing. Besides, he was dealing with ghosts. Who knew if any mortal weapon would really work against them? All he could think to do was to look as fearsome as possible and try to chase them away.

It didn't work.

And it wasn't necessarily because of the rope. It was because, just as Andy drew close to the horrifying creatures, he heard a loud, familiar voice behind him shout, *"Cut!"*

The ghosts halted where they were and looked inquiringly at the source of the interruption. Andy and Abigail stared, too, and were surprised to see Bartlemore standing there, looking completely at ease.

Bartlemore grinned and walked over to Andy. He took the rope from Andy's hands and tucked it beneath his arm.

"Thanks, I'll be needing that," Bartlemore said.

Andy stared, gobsmacked, as Bartlemore turned to

the three spirits and said, "That'll do. Now that we have the last two, phase one of the mission is over. You may return to your quarters."

The spirits nodded at Bartlemore and, without a sound, exited the room through a nearby tunnel.

"What's going on?" demanded Andy. "Who—or what—were those things?"

Bartlemore grinned. "They work for me. They're part of the Collective. Gifted stage magicians, all three."

Andy stared at Bartlemore. "Work for you? Wait. What are you saying?"

Bartlemore's trademark grin grew even wider. "What I'm saying, Andy Stanley, is that I have you trapped. I have imprisoned each of your companions, and now I have you and Abigail Awol, a naughty girl who is going to be severely punished for her betrayal."

Abigail's face paled. "Y-you're with the Collective? The famous John Bartlemore?"

Bartlemore snickered and said, "Hardly. The

real John Bartlemore is probably lounging by a pool surrounded by Hollywood starlets right now."

Suddenly, a haze seemed to pass over Bartlemore. To Andy, it felt like his eyes had gone blurry, almost like he were severely in need of a pair of glasses. As quickly as it appeared, the haze faded. In place of Bartlemore the actor stood Yaw Ripcord. She grinned, her full lips parted in a pink lipsticked smile.

Andy and Abigail couldn't believe their eyes. Yaw seemed to enjoy their stunned looks and let loose a rich, throaty laugh.

"Fun, isn't it? Wonder how it's done? Nothing up my sleeve . . ." She pulled up the sleeve of her blouse in imitation of a stage magician.

It was Abigail who put two and two together. "You've had it all along, haven't you?"

Yaw gave her a smug smile. "Yes, and you were all too dumb to realize it. Especially this new Keymaster everyone has been talking about."

She stared at Andy condescendingly. "You were so

easily convinced that your leader, Rusty Bucketts, was a spy. How in the world could the great Ned Lostmore put his faith in such a stupid boy? You'll never become a full Jungle Explorers' Society member believing everything you're told and turning on your friends."

Andy felt his cheeks grow hot with shame.

Abigail spoke up in his defense, saying, "He's new and was just trying to do what was right. You manipulated him, getting him to trust you as insurance so that you could stay close. Those 'traps' were put there by you, weren't they?"

"Of course they were," Yaw snapped. She gestured to the walls with open arms. "All of this was created by us, a trap to lure you here and get you out of the way. What better way than making you think you'd found the location of the Golden Paw? And perfectly safe, since I've had it all along."

"B-but where did you find it? What about the temple and those legends that Cedric told us about?"

Yaw shrugged. "Lies. I found the Golden Paw in a

place far from here, somewhere that's not on any map."
She called over her shoulder, "Cedric, would you come
here, please?"

Andy and Abigail watched as Cedric, wearing his
mask, emerged from a nearby passage. It was getting
hard for Andy to process all that he was seeing. It
seemed as if the entire world had turned upside down.

"I saw you die," Andy blurted.

Cedric held up a finger. "No, you didn't. You saw me
fall. Each of those pits you were so worried about is a
chute, conveniently placed so that we could eliminate
members of the group one by one. Taking you all on at
once would be a waste of time and, er—well, dash it all,
a waste of bodies. Everyone knows how well you fight
as a team. I was there on your last mission, remember?"

"You're the spy!" Andy exclaimed.

"Give the boy a gold star. He finally got one right,"
Yaw said. She clapped her hands in mock appreciation.

Cedric slipped off his mask and revealed his face
for the first time. Andy was shocked to see a mousy

man with large front teeth and a pencil-thin mustache standing before him.

"I worked for your grandfather for a while, but the Potentate gave me a better offer. She's set me up with all the medicines a poisoner could want. I can finally put my dark magic to good use."

"But you g-gave me those crocodile teeth," Andy stammered.

"Yes, by Jove, you're correct," Cedric said enthusiastically. Then his face fell. "But since you're still here, you obviously didn't use them as I instructed. They'd have killed you on the spot, dear chap."

Andy was suddenly thankful that he'd never opened the jar and obeyed the prescription given to him by Cedric the day they'd met.

"So the others are alive, too? Betty and Dotty? Rusty?" Abigail asked.

"For now," Yaw said. "Until I have no further use for them. It might take time, but thanks to dear old Cedric here, I have a machine that is capable of extracting information. Soon, all the secrets of the Jungle Explorers' Society will belong to us." She grinned. "It was so easy. Too easy, in fact. As Bartlemore, I got you moving, always irritating Bucketts to keep you from resting. As Yaw, I flew you to where I needed you to go. Didn't you notice that Bartlemore and Yaw were never in the same place at the same time?"

"But what about at Trader Sam's? Bartlemore's plane?" Andy asked.

"I had an associate fly it over. Then I left Rusty to fly from Trader Sam's alone while I changed back into Bartlemore. When I had an opportunity to get you alone, I seized it."

She reached into the pocket of her flight jacket and removed something that Andy recognized immediately.

"My Zoomwriter!"

Yaw laughed. "I could hardly believe my eyes when I saw it sitting on the counter at Trader Sam's. So careless to leave such a valuable item behind. . . ."

Andy's elation over seeing his pen evaporated. It

was bad enough to have it nearly within reach and not be able to touch it, but to know that it was in possession of his enemies was torture!

"Wait a minute. You keep talking about Yaw as if she were one of your disguises," Abigail said. Her eyes narrowed as she studied the woman in front of her. "Who are you *really*?"

"Smart girl. Yaw was simply an appearance I borrowed to gain the Society's trust. I am the Potentate," the woman said. "And who I really am isn't for you to know. Unlike the pathetic society of which you are a part, we keep our secrets."

She turned to Cedric. "You know what to do. Now that we have our prisoners, continue with the rest of the plan."

Cedric nodded. "How many soldiers should I take with me?"

The Potentate paused to think, then replied, "I should say six at least. He's bound to be well protected."

Cedric bowed. He turned to leave and then hesitated.

"After we have the information we need, shall I eliminate him?"

The Potentate gave him a mysterious, knowing smile. "Of course," she purred.

Cedric grinned in a way that made Andy feel very uncomfortable. What was he planning? Whatever it was, Andy could tell that something terrible was in store for them.

As Cedric strode from the chamber, the Potentate called after him.

"Cedric!"

"Yes, ma'am?"

Andy watched as she removed from her neck a slim golden chain with a claw-shaped pendant hanging from it. The minute she did, her form shimmered, turning from Yaw Ripcord's into that of a tall raven-haired woman wearing a silken mask.

It was the first time that Andy had seen the Golden Paw up close. It seemed to pulse with invisible power, making the tiny hairs on his arms and neck stand at attention. He'd been around magic enough now to recognize its signature feeling, and he could tell that, like the Pailina Pendant, this artifact held tremendous dark power.

The woman handed the Golden Paw to Cedric, who carefully took it from her and placed it in his pocket.

"You'll need it to gain access to him. Although we have his most formidable members, he's sure to be protected by others."

Wait a minute! Andy thought, putting two and two together. *She's . . . she's talking about Grandfather!*

Suddenly, it all made sense. Cedric was going to find Ned Lostmore and extract all the Jungle Explorers' Society's secrets from him. Worse still, Andy realized that when Cedric was done, he was going to kill him!

I've got to get out of here! Grandfather needs my help!

His blood boiling, Andy rushed toward Cedric, intending to tackle him to the ground. He was angrier than he'd ever been before and needed to get the Golden Paw away from him. With it, Cedric could impersonate anyone at all—even Andy himself! His poor grandfather would be caught unawares by the sneak attack!

But before he got to Cedric, the Potentate snapped her fingers, and several tough-looking men rushed into the chamber and grabbed Andy by the arms. He struggled as hard as he could.

"Let me go! You'll never get away with this!"

"Tie the two of them up with this," said the Potentate, indicating Andy and Abigail with a jerk of her head. She handed Andy's rope to the closest man, a hulking brute with a scar over one eye. "Put them with their friends. They're in for quite a reunion."

Chapter Seventeen
The Prison

It was more than an ordinary prison. It wasn't on any map and had been cleverly crafted to prevent escape. In fact, the ingenuity that had been employed by the dungeon's designer, a renowned torturer, had seen to it that the prison was filled with traps so nefarious any prisoner who tried to escape would encounter obstacles that would terrify the other captives into not even trying.

Long ago, the worst pirates that the Royal Navy had ever encountered had been placed there. Now Andy awoke in one of its cells. The Potentate's henchman had shoved a rough cloth soaked with some kind of chemical over his nose and mouth. Beyond that, he couldn't remember much. His head hurt. Everything hurt. He felt as if someone had hit him over and over with a sledgehammer.

Worse than the pain he felt was the knowledge that Ned was in danger, and there was nothing he could do about it.

Andy gazed at his surroundings with mounting despair. The dungeon walls were made of thick, impenetrable stone, except for the entrance to his cell, which was made of heavy iron bars. Abigail wasn't anywhere in sight. Neither were the rest of his friends.

Andy felt dizzy as he rose from the chilly flagstone floor. He stumbled over to the bars and, gripping them with both hands, called out, "Hello? Is anybody there?"

"Andy? Is that you?" came a familiar voice from somewhere down the outside corridor.

"Rusty! You're alive!" Andy said.

"Barely, boy. Barely," Rusty said. Andy noticed that his normally booming voice sounded tired and weak.

"Are the others okay? What about Betty and Dotty?"

"We're here," said two voices in unison.

"Okay, but not great," Dotty added.

"I'm here, too," Abigail called. "I feel like I was thrown in here like a rag doll after they drugged me."

The Collective will pay for that, Andy thought. *And for what they've done to the others, too. When I find a way out of here, I'm going to get my Zoomwriter back and get us all free.*

"We've got to get out of here," Andy called. "Ned is in danger!"

He related to the others what he'd heard with Abigail. They all agreed he'd come to the correct conclusion based on the cryptic conversation the Potentate had had with Cedric.

"Why, that double-crossing little quack!" Rusty growled. "When I get my hands on that tribal-masked fiend, he's going to wish he'd never been born."

Betty, Dotty, and Abigail voiced similar convictions. To have one of their own betray the Society like this was the worst thing anyone could imagine. Each of them owed Ned Lostmore a great debt, and all considered him a dear friend. But to Andy, it went deeper than that. Ned was family! He couldn't allow anything to happen to him.

Andy tugged on the bars with all his might. Truthfully, he hadn't expected much to happen. To his surprise, the door to his cell swung open easily.

"Hey!" Andy shouted. "They forgot to lock my door!"

"Don't move!" Rusty shouted back. "It's a trap!"

Andy poked his head out of the cell door. All he could see was a long hallway with a trench of murky water flowing down the center of it. There didn't seem to be anything dangerous.

"But there's nothing there," Andy said.

"This place is known in the criminal underworld. If we are where I think we are, most of them call it Prisoner's Folly. Nobody knows the original name. It might never have even had one. . . . I heard about it when my plane was grounded with engine trouble in the Caribbean. Had to spend the night in a very sketchy inn, a place I wouldn't recommend to anyone," Rusty said in a pained voice.

"It looks like an ordinary dungeon to me," Andy replied.

"Trust me, it's not," said Rusty. "Every prisoner is given the opportunity to escape. I think it's mostly for the entertainment of the people who put us here. This place is designed to drive a person insane. If you think the traps that the Collective put in front of us in that phony Death Maze were bad, you have no idea what this place can do."

Andy stared down the hallway at the place where he thought Rusty was imprisoned. He couldn't see him, but he could hear his voice. Aside from the muddied trench, the corridor looked clean and well cared for. How in the world could it be dangerous to at least have a look around outside his cell?

"Hey, Rusty, are you sure? I mean, how do you know that this is Prisoner's Folly? What if we're just in an old dungeon somewhere?"

"Because I tried leaving my cell," said Rusty. "And look what it did to me."

Down the hall, Andy saw a meaty arm poke out from the farthest cell. But an arm was all that he saw. Where Rusty's left hand used to be was nothing but a stump covered with bloody rags.

Andy felt sick. "What did that to you?"

"So far as I can tell, it was a Dingonek," said Rusty. "It's a legendary creature that can only be summoned using the talisman of Magu Wandu. It's part crocodile, part scorpion, and a hundred percent vicious. The minute you set foot on those flagstones, a door opens at the end of the hall and the beast is released. It came swimming at me down that trench quicker than lightning. Nothing I could do to stop it."

Andy paled. He'd almost charged right out of his cell without thinking!

"Will you be okay?" Abigail called.

"Just a scratch," Rusty replied bravely. But Andy could tell by the sound of his voice that he was in a lot of pain.

Think, Andy, think. This can't be the end. There's got to be a way out of here....

Andy gazed around his cell, inspecting everything closely. He moved over to the rocks on the wall and began to meticulously scan them for any anomalies. He'd read about prisoners sometimes leaving messages for other prisoners who might be put in the same cell. Perhaps one of the pirates who used to be imprisoned there had done the same.

The first wall he looked at yielded nothing. But while on his hands and knees in the far corner of the cell, he saw something worth noting.

The mortar around this stone looks like it's crumbled away. It was exactly the kind of thing that he was looking for!

Andy held his breath as he tried to work the small

stone free, desperately hoping that his instincts were leading him down the right track. After all, pirates were good at hiding treasure, weren't they? Couldn't one of them have hidden a message behind the stone?

His fingertips grew scraped and bloodied as he worked, but hope kept him at it. Finally, after several minutes, there was a small *pop* and the stone came free.

Andy probed the spot where the stone had been. At first he didn't think anything was there. Then his fingers brushed something in the farthest recesses of the hole. He strained to grab it.

Andy's pulse quickened when he saw what he'd found. It was a tiny piece of leather wrapped with a bit of thread.

"I found something," he called out.

"What?" came Abigail's reply.

"I think it might be a message from one of the former prisoners," Andy said. He fumbled with the thread and, after breaking it with his teeth, unrolled the tiny piece of leather. There were words written there in brown ink!

Old blood, more like. Andy knew about all kinds of different inks because of his fascination with fountain pens. This wasn't like any ink he'd ever seen. Besides, a prisoner wouldn't have access to much. Whoever had been there before him had probably had to make do with what was at hand.

Andy read the message written there first to himself. Then, unable to contain his excitement, he read it aloud to the others. Some of the message was faded, but Andy felt that there was enough there to figure out the note.

"Beware ye the devil in the deep," Andy read. *"For she'll surely take yer life.*

She cannae be harmed by mortal strength,
but obeys the shipwright's fife.
Barnacle Billy took it below;
he's in the Rog Guffaw.
So if ye dare to take a swim,
beware the creature's maw."

"What's it mean?" Betty called out.

"I really don't know," Andy confessed.

"It's got to be code for something," said Abigail.

Andy racked his brain, trying to figure out the meaning behind the rhyme. He was good with riddles and secret codes, but this one was different from most. It seemed like this one was less about figuring out a puzzle and more like understanding the language that the writer was using.

Okay, let me try taking it line by line, he thought. He gazed at the scrap of leather, going over the words carefully.

Beware ye the devil in the deep. Well, that one was easy enough. In this case, the writer of the poem was definitely referring to the monster in the water.

For she'll surely take yer life. Again, pretty obvious. Rusty's injury was testimony to what the terrible creature could do if she caught you. Andy grimaced as he thought about the possibility of his friend bleeding to death.

Poor Rusty. He needs to see a doctor!

Andy tried to put his anxiety out of his mind and

concentrate instead on the task at hand. He breathed deeply to steady himself and read on.

She cannae be harmed by mortal strength,

but obeys the shipwright's fife.

What was a shipwright's fife? Andy stared at the phrase, trying to figure it out.

Abigail interrupted his thoughts. "I've got an idea!" she called.

"What?" Andy called back.

"I was thinking about the words. *Shipwright.* That's a carpenter who builds boats. But why would a carpenter be playing a fife? Isn't a fife a small flute? It doesn't make sense unless it has to do with being on a ship. Is there a special instrument associated with being on a boat?"

Andy tried to think about all the books he'd read about sailing, like the Horatio Hornblower novels and *Treasure Island.* Was there anything mentioned there?

Ok, let's think about this. Is there another name for a shipwright? What are the positions on a ship? There's the captain, of course. He has a first mate. The person who steers is the helmsman. And the ship's carpenter is a . . .

"A boatswain!" Andy exclaimed. Then the other part of the phrase made sense. The boatswain had his own special instrument for calling the crew to attention.

"I've got part of it," he called. "*The shipwright's fife* refers to a boatswain's whistle," Andy said excitedly. "It's a funny-looking brass whistle that's usually worn on a chain around the carpenter's neck."

"Good job, Andy!" called Abigail. The others gave a weak cheer.

"That means that this creature—what did you call it?" Andy asked.

"Dingonek," Rusty called.

"The Dingonek must be sensitive to its sound. It says in the poem that it obeys the shipwright's fife. Maybe the person who discovered that escaped, but hid this note for the next person imprisoned here to find."

"But where is it? Is there any boatswain's whistle hidden in your cell?" called Dotty.

"I don't think so," Andy said. He glanced over the poem again. "It says, *Barnacle Billy took it below; he's in the Rog Guffaw.*"

"Could it mean that whoever Barnacle Billy is, he's buried beneath one of the cells?" Abigail asked.

Andy shook his head. "I have a feeling that *below* refers to the water." He glanced uneasily at the deep channel of water that flowed down the chamber outside his cell.

"Okay, but if that's the case, then what's the Rog Guffaw? It sounds like a location," said Betty.

"Maybe," said Andy. "Let me think some more."

Rog Guffaw, Rog Guffaw. Andy couldn't remember hearing that name in any story about ships. What could a Rog Guffaw be? And how could someone be *in* it?

He gazed at the poem and tried separating the words. Rog. It could sound like *log*. Or maybe it was short for something. *Reg* could be short for *regius* and was also an abbreviation for the name Reggie. What if Rog didn't sound like *log*, but *Raj*, like short for . . . ?

"Roger," Andy whispered. "Okay, now if *Rog* is short

for *Roger*, how could Billy be *in* the Roger Guffaw? Unless . . ."

Andy brightened. Of course! It was so simple! *Guffaw* was another word for laughter. But in pirate speak, *Rog Guffaw* could mean . . .

"Jolly Roger!" Andy exclaimed. "Barnacle Billy must have died and been wrapped in a pirate flag, commonly called the Jolly Roger. And since they couldn't bury him at sea like pirates usually do, they must have dumped him in . . ."

Andy's voice trailed off as he gazed at the horrible trench. Somewhere down at the bottom of the trench was the ship's carpenter, the boatswain called Barnacle Billy. The pirate who had left the note wouldn't have wanted to risk his captors finding the boatswain's whistle after he escaped. So he'd hidden it on Billy's bones under the water.

Andy gulped. The rest of the poem was easy now.

So if ye dare to take a swim,

beware the creature's maw.

Andy knew *maw* referred to the jaws or throat of a voracious animal. Now everything was clear. He knew what he had to do.

"Looks like I'm going for a swim!"

Chapter Eighteen
The Dingonek

Andy stood, shivering, at the edge of his cell. He'd stripped down to his skivvies so that his clothes would stay dry.

"Andy, be careful! Are you sure you want to do this? What if the note isn't true?" Abigail asked.

Andy called back, "It's the only chance we've got."

Suddenly, a noise that sounded like booted feet echoed on the ceiling above them.

"It's the guards," Betty and Dotty said in unison.

Andy knew there was no time to waste. "I'm going in," he said. "If I don't make it back, please do everything you can to rescue my grandfather."

"Andy, wait!" Abigail shouted.

But Andy ignored her. After taking a couple of steadying breaths, he leapt from the cell and ran as fast as he could to the deep trench in the center of the hall. As he ran, he heard the sound of a heavy door scraping open from somewhere and a huge splash.

Don't think about it!

Andy hit the water. When it came to athletics, he wasn't all that gifted. He wasn't a particularly strong swimmer, but he knew he could hold his own.

Andy kicked his feet like his life depended on it—which it probably did. He had no idea where the Dingonek was, and he cringed at the thought of its powerful jaws closing on his feet. The water in the trench was murky, but he could make out shapes beneath the surface. He dove deeper, hoping beyond hope that he'd deciphered the note correctly.

His lungs were screaming for air when he spotted what he was looking for—a black flag wrapped around a bulky form. He could see the hint of a skull and cross-bones along one side.

Barnacle Billy!

Andy kicked hard to the surface and grabbed a quick breath before diving back down again. Fearful that the Dingonek's sharp teeth might pierce his legs at any minute, he tore away the rotted fabric that covered the bones and searched desperately around the skeleton's neck for the chain a boatswain usually hung his whistle upon. There was nothing there! Then, just as he was about to give up hope, he felt the tiny links of a chain stuck between two of the neck verte-brae of the skeleton.

Andy gave a mighty tug. The chain was stuck! If he couldn't get it soon, he would be out of air!

A shadow passed over the skeleton. Andy looked up and saw that a gigantic pair of eyes were suddenly even with his. The Dingonek was a monster unlike anything

Andy had ever seen before. Its face reminded him vaguely of an anglerfish, with horrible pale eyes and long saberlike teeth that stuck out from its lower jaw. But the resemblance stopped there. On its head stood a large pointed horn, and its tail was barbed like that of a scorpion!

The sight filled Andy with such horror that, without even thinking, he jerked back on the chain he was holding. The skeleton's bones cracked and the whistle came free.

The Dingonek lunged, its mouth open wide like a great white shark's. Andy, driven by adrenaline and fear, ducked under the creature at the last possible second. He barely managed to avoid the stinger tail as he swam beneath its belly.

He was screaming bloody murder inside, terrified to death of the creature. But the extra boost of adrenaline that the fear gave him enabled him to kick harder and swim faster than he ever had before in his life!

Andy broke the surface with a huge shuddering

gasp. He wasted no time in leaping over the edge of the trench. Scrambling on all fours like a frightened crab, he raced toward his cell. He was dimly aware of figures standing at the end of the hallway, pistols drawn, but he didn't have time to think about them. The Dingonek was amphibious, and it leapt right out of the water. It was hot on his heels, its gigantic crocodile-like form slamming down on the flagstones just inches from his left foot!

Andy knew he would never make it to his cell in time. The creature was faster than he was and, as evidenced by Rusty's arm, would bite him in two the first chance it got.

He fumbled with the chain and raised the boatswain's whistle to his lips. At first, there was no noise other than water bursting through the hole. But then a high, piercing note rang through the prison corridor.

Andy heaved and collapsed on the floor. Blowing the whistle had taken every last ounce of breath he had possessed. He glanced behind him and saw that he'd deciphered the poem correctly. The Dingonek, huge and terrible, was writhing on the ground, gnashing its terrible jaws. A second later, it began to shimmer. And then, with a golden burst of light, it disappeared, leaving behind what looked like an ancient amulet.

"Get the artifact!" a voice shouted. Three guards rushed toward it, but Andy lunged for it just before they got there.

"Back off!" he shouted. "Or I'll release it again, and this time it's going for you!"

The guards hesitated, their eyes round with fear. A man dressed in a military jacket and goggles, who Andy could only assume was their leader, said, "Give it here, sonny. That belongs to us!"

"N-not anymore," Andy said. His teeth had started to chatter because of the trauma and the chilly dungeon. "Get back and throw down your weapons."

The leader nodded to the others, who tossed their pistols on the ground. They all backed up several feet, evidently terrified of Andy's threat. Andy had no idea how to activate the amulet that summoned the Dingonek, but he didn't want them to know that.

"Rusty, Betty, Dotty, Abigail, if you could help, please, I'd appreciate it," Andy called.

His friends exited their cells, wide-eyed and impressed with Andy's feat of courage. In spite of his weak condition, Rusty quickly gathered the pistols, keeping one and tossing the others to Betty and Dotty.

Andy nodded and ducked into his cell, eager to get his dry clothes back on. He shivered violently as he pulled on his shirt, trousers, and jacket. Inside, he felt triumphant. He'd accomplished something that had been nearly impossible!

While Rusty ushered the guards into one of the cells, Betty and Dotty found an old lock. The twins gagged and bound the prisoners with tattered rags that they'd discovered in a couple of old barrels, then locked the cell door.

Abigail rushed over to Andy and threw her arms around his neck.

"That was one of the bravest things I've ever seen anyone do in my whole life," she whispered. "I'm glad you made it."

Then, suddenly, she kissed his cheek, and Andy felt all the coldness disappear as a warm glow suffused his cheeks.

Chapter Nineteen
The Dead End

ortunately, the guards had left the door through which they'd entered unlocked. Andy knew Rusty was too weak to lead the group, so he volunteered to be first through the door.

"Stay close," he said. The others nodded. Perhaps it was because of the courage he'd shown when confronting the Dingonek, but the others seemed to sense a change in him and didn't question his leadership.

As they opened the heavy wooden door and went

cautiously through, Andy wished again that he had his Zoomwriter. He wondered where it was. Did the Potentate have it locked away in her private chambers? Or was it lying in a box somewhere with all their other belongings?

Based on the way the leader of the Collective had recognized the pen's value, Andy guessed that she probably kept it somewhere close at hand. He vowed that he would get it back from her—if he ever got the chance.

Beyond the wooden door lay a dimly lit hallway. Andy assumed that it was the same hallway that they'd all been dragged through when he and the others had been put in their cells. After ascending some steep stone stairs, they passed a room that looked like guards' quarters. And then the passageway they'd been following stopped, abruptly ending in a wall of stone. Andy looked around. There had to be an entrance for the guards to come through. But try as he might, he couldn't see anything.

"Where to now?" Abigail asked.

"I don't know. There should be a door somewhere. Maybe it's a secret entrance," Andy said. "Everybody try looking for something that looks slightly out of place. It might be a stone without mortar around it, or a hidden switch."

They scoured the walls. But after several minutes of searching, they still hadn't found anything. On an impulse, Andy went back to the small room that seemed to be the guards' quarters. Looking around, he saw a pair of iron bunk beds, a fireplace, a rough-hewn table, a small pile of rations, and a rather dull knife.

"Not much here," he murmured. But then he spotted something out of place on the mantel above the blackened hearth. Hope flaring in his chest, he called back to the others, who were still searching the dead-end passage.

"I think I might have found something!"

The group filed into the small, dank room. Andy grinned. "Notice anything strange about this room?"

The others glanced around. Betty wrinkled her nose. "It smells like old socks."

"Besides that," Andy said.

"Looks like an ordinary setup to me," Rusty said. "Typical soldiers' quarters. Not too different from the battalion quarters I had back in the war." He winced and held his injured arm.

Andy was reminded again that Rusty needed medical attention and decided it would be better to just reveal what he'd found rather than drag it out. He walked over to the fireplace mantel and pointed at the bookends that were positioned upon it. They held an old book between them, something titled *Beecham's Guide to Butterfly Collecting*.

"Unusual reading for soldier types, don't you think?" Andy asked.

The bookends on either side of the book were mismatched. One of them was carved into the shape of a bird taking flight, while the other resembled a pyramid with an all-seeing eye on top of it.

Without hesitating, Andy pulled the book forward. As he'd expected, it swiveled on a hinge. It wasn't a real book at all, but a switch.

The fireplace rotated back to reveal a spiral staircase.

"Well done!" Abigail said.

"Keep your weapons at the ready," Andy said. "We have no idea what we might find up there."

This time, Betty and Dotty, who each held a pistol, led the way. Andy followed behind them, and Abigail brought up the rear with Rusty. Andy counted the stairs as they went up. He had just reached 125 when he found himself on a flat landing. Everyone, especially Rusty, was out of breath from the exertion, and the group paused before opening the plain door at the top.

With a little luck, there won't be anybody waiting for us behind the door.

Andy braced himself as Betty and Dotty turned the knob and pushed it open. Thankfully, there wasn't any exclamation of surprise when it swung open. The room they entered was empty. But it also looked very peculiar.

Peering over Betty and Dotty's shoulder, Andy saw a scarred wooden floor with two identical rustic doors made from slats of bamboo on the opposite wall. Aside from the doors and a lone candelabra, the room was empty.

"Strange," Betty said.

"Yes," Andy said. "I don't like it." There was something about the doors that reminded him of stories he'd read where the hero had to make a choice. One door usually led to freedom, and the other to certain death.

He hoped that wasn't the case with these doors.

"Should we try one?" Abigail asked.

"We'll have to choose. I have a feeling that we'll only get one chance. If the rumors about this dungeon are true, then the Collective probably knows which door to use and which one an escaping prisoner might mistakenly walk through," Andy said.

Andy walked closer and inspected both doors. Even with his meticulous eye for detail, he couldn't see a single difference between them.

"Hogwash," Rusty said. "I'd wager that neither of them is dangerous. One's probably a closet."

But Andy had a strong sense of foreboding. Something just didn't feel right. Before he could again express the need for caution, Rusty stepped forward and twisted the knob on the left door with his good hand.

The floor began to shake.

"Back to the staircase!" Andy yelled.

But he hadn't taken a single step before the solid-looking marble beneath their feet cracked like thin ice. Andy felt his foot slip through the floor. The next thing he knew, the ground had crumbled away and they were all screaming in terror as they fell down, down, down into darkness.

Chapter Twenty
The Horrible Isnashi

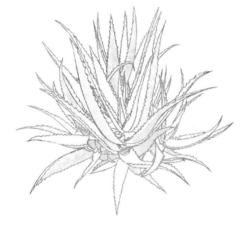

They landed in an unceremonious heap. Fortunately, their fall was broken by several gigantic ferns. Unfortunately, as Andy found out at that moment, not all ferns are soft, and some of them possess particularly nasty thorns.

Still, with the exception of some bumps, scratches, and bruises, everyone seemed to be okay. Only Rusty hadn't fared well. He was already weak from his encounter with the Dingonek, and between the fall, the rough landing, and the loss of blood he'd suffered, he appeared to be unconscious.

"We've got to do something!" Abigail said, noting the big man's gray pallor.

"If we had our pack, we could help him," Betty said. "We always carry a first aid kit. But other than trying to make him as comfortable as we can, I'm afraid there's not much we can do."

The sisters looked worried. Dotty folded her silk sash into a makeshift pillow and placed it beneath the bush pilot's head.

"Maybe there *is* something," Andy said. He gazed around at their new surroundings. They'd landed in an immense cavern filled with plant life. High above was an opening that allowed daylight to shine down, giving the plants the sunlight and rain that they needed to survive.

And survive they had. In fact, the foliage had

flourished. Andy could tell at a glance that these weren't just jungle plants. There was an entire forest of deciduous trees and flowers.

"Maybe there are some medicinal plants around here," Abigail suggested.

"Good idea," Andy said. "I learned about some of them in Boy Scouts. I'll be right back."

"Be careful," Abigail warned. "We have no idea what might be lurking in this place."

Andy nodded and determinedly set off toward a nearby grove of thickly clustered palm trees. There were several desert plants in the area, and after searching for a bit, Andy found what he was looking for—a large aloe vera plant.

Why is it purple, though? Every aloe plant he'd ever seen was green. Andy shrugged and broke off several fronds, pocketing a few and carrying the rest.

When Andy brought them back to the others and showed them what he'd found, Betty's and Dotty's eyes immediately widened.

"Where did you find purple aloe?" Dotty asked.

Andy gestured to the area. "Over by those palms. I was looking for regular aloe, but I found this stuff. It's not poisonous, is it?"

Betty laughed. "Poisonous? Are you kidding? Purple aloe has miraculous healing powers. It's incredibly rare! You couldn't have found anything better!"

Betty and Dotty took the fronds that Andy had been carrying. Then, unwrapping Rusty's makeshift bandage, the sisters applied the sap to the open wound. Betty rewrapped the injury using Dotty's sash, tightening it like a tourniquet above Rusty's wrist to prevent further blood loss.

"He's going to be all right now," Dotty said. "Purple aloe works very quickly! I've seen it used once before, and the patient was up on his feet in minutes."

Andy gazed around at the thick vegetation. "Maybe we're lucky that we found this place. It seems like every imaginable plant is growing here."

Abigail was about to respond when a loud roar

echoed from somewhere near where they were sitting. They shared nervous glances.

"We're not alone," Betty said.

"Not at all," Dotty echoed.

"That didn't sound like any creature I've ever heard," Abigail said. "Not a lion, for sure."

"You two had better have your pistols ready," Andy suggested. "Whatever that was, it sounded pretty close."

The trees shook with the creature's unearthly roar as whatever it was stomped in their direction. Andy and the others had no idea what to expect, but they could feel the ground shake beneath their feet with every thunderous footfall. Then a terrible stench like a cross between rotten eggs and a skunk filled the air.

"Hide!" Andy shouted.

"What about Rusty?" Abigail asked.

"Help me drag him," Andy said. "Betty, Dotty, you guys take cover in that big bush over there. We'll hide behind that tree. Maybe we can take it by surprise."

Rusty was heavy, and trying to move him felt to

Andy like pulling a sack filled with boulders. But with much heaving and grunting, he and Abigail managed to get the bush pilot and themselves hidden behind a big-trunked eucalyptus tree just as the creature burst into the clearing they'd recently occupied.

The moment Andy laid eyes on it, his stomach churned. It was one of the most horrible creatures that he'd ever seen—even worse than most of the mythical monsters he'd read about.

It didn't seem possible. The monster had thick, matted fur and strode upon two legs like a gorilla. But the resemblance ended there. Like a Cyclops, it had a single eye—one that was inky black, with no white at all—and upon its belly was a wide, gaping slash filled with broken teeth.

Its mouth is on its stomach! Andy realized. It just looked wrong!

"It's an Isnashi!" whispered Abigail.

"A what-she?" said Andy.

"Isnashi! My father told me about them. I . . . I didn't

think they were real. He said he barely escaped one when he was on an expedition in Brazil, but I thought he was making it up."

"Evidently not," Andy said.

The beast swayed in place for a moment, sniffing the air as if deciding which way it should turn. The stench of the thing at close proximity was overwhelming, and Andy had a hard time not gagging.

Andy saw Betty and Dotty peer over the top of the large bush they were hiding behind, taking aim with their pistols.

Don't miss, Andy begged silently. *Please . . . don't miss.*

The sisters fired, but the Isnashi was quicker. At the last possible moment, the beast leapt into the air, avoiding the bullets and landing directly behind the twins!

Betty and Dotty weren't easily frightened, and if the sudden proximity of the horrible monster bothered them, they didn't show it. With lightning reflexes, the twins responded. The two let fly a quick series of karate punches, followed by powerful leaping roundhouse kicks.

The women were masters of the martial arts, and they sang as they fought, harmonizing a battle song of their own composition. Andy had heard it once before, when they'd battled the Collective in Hawaii. The music Betty and Dotty made together was beautiful, with an eerie quality about it. It reminded Andy vaguely of the drone of a bagpipe coupled with its high, lilting melody.

It inspired fear in any enemy that heard it.

The assault from the conjoined twins would have knocked any normal opponent back at least thirty feet, and the fierce song they sang would have made the foe think twice about continuing the fight. But the Isnashi was anything but normal.

The sisters stood facing a foe that had barely moved under their best assault, and a flicker of doubt passed between them. When Andy saw that look, he knew that if he didn't do something quick, Betty and Dotty, the fiercest fighters he knew, probably wouldn't survive.

Andy glanced around desperately, hoping to see a club or a sharp stick lying nearby. But deep inside, he knew that such weapons would be pointless. And then he remembered. He still had the amulet that had summoned the Dingonek!

Andy reached into his jacket pocket and pulled it out. He scanned the surface of the amulet, looking for anything at all that would tell him how to summon the creature. There was a skull on one side and a smooth surface on the other, but nothing was written there.

The Isnashi loomed over Betty and Dotty, its horrible mouth gaping, ready to bite. Andy rubbed hard on the amulet with his thumb, polishing its surface and trying to see if perhaps the thin layer of grime had obscured some faintly written text.

There was nothing written on the amulet, but as with the fabled genie in Aladdin's lamp, it was the rubbing that did the trick. Andy gasped as the amulet suddenly grew white-hot. He tossed it on the ground and watched as the amulet began to spin. There was a shimmer and then, uncurling like a great crocodile, the Dingonek reappeared. Andy didn't have to tell it what to do. The creature obeyed the intention of whoever was in control of the amulet.

The Dingonek roared, and the Isnashi, for the first time in its miserable existence, faced an opponent that was a true challenge. It seemed to know right away that it was threatened, and it let loose another of its terrible howls. The monsters rushed together and fought, a clash of two creatures straight out of myth and legend.

Had it been something in the movies, Andy would have been riveted to the spot. But seeing it for real was truly terrible to behold. Both creatures were fighting for their lives!

The Dingonek's barbed tail struck over and over again, and the Isnashi, brandishing a set of huge scimitar-like claws, slashed back. There was blood everywhere.

"Come on," hissed Abigail. "While they're distracted, we need to find a way out of here!"

Andy shook his head, clearing his mind. "You're right." He glanced down at Rusty. "But what about him? We can't just leave him here."

Abigail reached down and lightly tapped Rusty's cheek. "Rusty, wake up! We're in danger! Wake up!"

Rusty's eyes flickered and he let out a small moan.

"He's awake!" Andy said.

The big man slowly sat up, his good hand clutching his injured arm.

"What's happening?" he asked.

"No time to explain," Abigail said. "We've got to get out of here. Can you walk?"

Rusty nodded and stumbled to his feet. Andy noticed that the color had returned to his cheeks, and he looked close to his old self.

That purple aloe works wonders!

Rusty glanced over at the vicious fight going on between the Isnashi and the Dingonek. His eyes widened.

"Where's my pistol?" he growled.

"It won't work," Andy said quickly. He motioned for

Betty and Dotty to follow. The twins rushed over from behind the bush where they'd been watching the battle of the two titans.

"How do we get out of here?" Abigail asked.

"I have an idea," Andy said. He glanced in the direction the first howl of the Isnashi had come from.

"Follow me!"

Chapter Twenty-One
The Cave

ndy and the others found what they were looking for easily enough, as the stench of the creature was as obvious as a series of arrows painted on the ground. It got stronger as they reached the Isnashi's dwelling and was nearly overpowering once they were inside of the cave.

From the skeletal remains that littered the floor of the Isnashi's cave, it seemed few people—if any—had ever made it out of the monster's lair alive. Hidden behind the bones, deep inside the fetid dwelling, was an ancient door.

Eyes watering and breathing through their noses to keep out the smell, Andy and the others waded through the bones and made their way to the door.

For all its brute strength, the Isnashi evidently wasn't very intelligent. The door had a primitive latch that, when thrown, opened easily enough.

The group wasted no time in going through the door and slamming it shut behind them. They gazed around at their new surroundings in awe. They were outside . . . back in the jungle they'd so recently been hiking through.

The air was damp but fresh, and all of them happily took in great lungfuls of the humid air.

Andy glanced back at the exit through which they'd come. The door to the Isnashi's cave had been carved into the side of a mountain. They'd found an escape in a very unlikely spot. It was one that Andy hoped was outside the knowledge of the Collective.

"This mountain looks familiar," said Rusty.

"I think we're near the entrance to the Death Maze," Abigail said. "The mountain looks the same. Maybe they didn't take us far when they drugged us."

"We've got to get to my grandfather," Andy said. "The last thing he told me was that he was going back to see Jack McGraw."

"Then he's probably at the Jungle Navigation Company docks. We'll need a boat," said Abigail.

Andy looked around. There was nothing but jungle in every direction. Then his eyes fell upon a very unusual tree. It was much taller and broader than the rest, and there seemed to be something built in its branches.

"Wait, what's that?" Andy asked. He pointed to the tree.

"What?" Abigail said. "That tree?"

"It doesn't look like an ordinary tree," Andy said. "Look, up there in its branches."

Rusty's eyes widened with surprise. "Crickets and cats! It looks like some kind of treehouse!"

"That's a *Yesniddendron semperflorens grandis*," Betty said.

"This must be one of the largest ever-blooming trees of its kind," Dotty added.

"Very rare," Betty concluded.

"Maybe there's someone up there who can help us," Andy suggested. "Come on."

Chapter Twenty-Two
The Treehouse

It was agreed that Rusty, Betty, and Dotty would stand guard at the base of the trunk while Andy and Abigail investigated the mysterious treehouse.

The base of the tree was huge, consisting of centuries-old twisted roots that tangled around each other. A staircase carved into the trunk of the tree led upward, its banister made of thick rope. Looking up, Andy saw that the stairs twisted high into the massive branches, disappearing at the top into an alcove on a particularly sturdy branch that looked to be about ten feet wide.

"Stay quiet," Andy said. "There might be someone up there. We don't want to alert the wrong people to our presence."

They did their best to walk as quietly as possible. It made climbing the big trunk take much longer than it ordinarily would have, but Andy wasn't about to take the risk of alerting anyone to their presence. At the top, he was amazed to discover a sprawling series of rooms installed beneath the leafy canopy of the tree.

I wonder what secrets are hiding up here?

Abigail must have been thinking the same thing, because she pointed at the nearest room with a surprised expression. Andy followed her gaze. The cleverly designed room had a maple writing desk and a reading lamp. Leaning against the far wall in the corner was something familiar.

"Those are our things!" Abigail whispered.

It was true. The rucksacks they'd been carrying before they were captured were neatly stacked against the wall.

The two made their way as quickly and quietly as they could to their gear. As they gathered everything up, Abigail leaned in close to Andy's ear and whispered, "Let's get out of here while we can."

"You go," Andy said. "I want to look around."

Abigail looked like she was about to protest, but thought better of it.

"Fine," she whispered. "I'll take these down to the others. Be careful!"

Andy nodded. After shouldering his own pack, he moved farther up the main branch to the next alcove. He glanced inside the closest room and noticed nothing interesting, just a kitchen with a huge clamshell for a sink. The next room down the branch had some beds and a hammock.

Since there was still no sign of anyone about, he went up to the last room at the top of the branch. This one was the largest, and when he looked inside, his breath caught in his throat.

It was a sumptuously arrayed office with several large maps on the walls. A pipe organ was installed in one corner of the room, and a huge walnut desk with elaborately carved legs stood in the other. A beautiful old record player—a gramophone with a large bluebell-colored horn—sat next to the desk.

As Andy scanned the room, his eyes fell on a glass dome on the desk. There was something beneath it—something instantly recognizable and almost painfully familiar.

My Zoomwriter!

Andy rushed over as quietly as he could. Removing the dome, he retrieved his pen and inspected the jade barrel and nib for any signs of damage.

There were none.

Andy could have shouted with glee! In a million years, he never would have thought he'd find it so easily. Of course, he never would have pictured its being held inside a treehouse, either. Having it back in his possession once more made him feel a strong sense of security.

Andy was about to leave the room when he noticed something else on the desk. Curious, he decided to hazard a closer look.

It was a drawing of an ancient-seeming clock. Instead of numbers, strange figures decorated its face. Looking closer, Andy saw that with each change of the hour, the figures grew progressively more tortured.

On hour one, the figure looked frightened. By hour three, he was covered in what looked like pestilent boils. At hour six, swarms of terrible insects streamed from the sky. By hour nine, the figure had grown thin, his eyes bulging in a manner that clearly indicated starvation.

The symbol depicted where the twelve should have been was the worst one of all: a grinning skull staring back at Andy with lifeless eyes. It didn't take much interpretation to figure out what that meant.

Death comes at midnight.

Andy shuddered and looked over the rest of the desk. Beside the image of the clock, on a separate piece of paper, was a series of notes. They had been hand-written in an elegant script that Andy realized with a pang of resentment had been written with his own pen. His Zoomwriter. He'd know the ink pigment and nib size anywhere!

As Andy read the notes, all the color drained from his face.

Instructions for finding and activating the Doomsday Device contained in Library of Alexandria. Key of Fate opens vault where last page is contained. Currently held by the J.E.S. Obtain key. Kill Lostmore.

"Doomsday Device?" Andy whispered. "That doesn't sound good."

Then he realized the extent of the Potentate's plan.

She had known that Ned had the key and had wanted to get Rusty and the rest of the group out of the way so that she could steal it. Whatever this "Doomsday Device" was, if the sketch was any indication, it was something terribly powerful. Possibly more powerful than any other artifact ever discovered.

Andy thought back to what his grandfather had told him when he'd brought him the key. How mysterious and important he'd said it was, and that what was written in the vault it protected could affect the safety of the entire world.

I've got to warn Grandfather that she's coming!

Andy folded up the drawing and the notes. After placing them in his rucksack, he rushed out of the room. As he was leaving, he suddenly paused. Looking out over the nearest banister, he caught sight of something in the far distance. From so great a height, he could see the entire jungle. Better yet, he could see the Amazon River. He saw a dock and several boats waiting in the harbor. Swarms of people were loading wooden crates onto one of the biggest boats. The men were clad in black, just like the thugs the Potentate commanded.

So that's why there's nobody around, Andy thought. *They're leaving this place to go search for the Doomsday Device!*

Andy rushed down the stairs two at time, knowing that he had to move fast if he was going to have any chance of rescuing his grandfather and stopping the Collective from destroying the world.

Chapter Twenty-Three
A Daring Escape

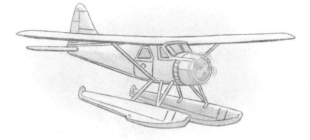

usty and the others wasted no time in following Andy's directions to the river dock. As they drew closer, the group prepared for the fight that was sure to come. Stealing a boat from under the noses of the Collective wasn't going to be a cakewalk. The highly trained criminals were sure to put up a ferocious fight.

Rusty retrieved his favorite weapon from his rucksack. But as he held up the slingshot he used to shoot his artificial ball-bearing eye, his expression changed.

Without the use of his other hand, a slingshot would be useless.

"Maybe you should stick to the pistol," Andy suggested.

Andy felt sorry for Rusty, but if the sturdy bush pilot was feeling sorry for himself, he didn't show it. He tossed the slingshot back in his pack and grabbed the pistol instead. "An amateur's weapon" was all he said. And Andy could tell by the note of disgust in his voice that he thought very little of using guns.

Betty and Dotty had retrieved their katanas and throwing stars. The twins began a series of stretching exercises to limber up for the fight.

Andy's stomach was in knots. It wasn't just that they were horribly outnumbered. It was that with every second that went by, he worried that he would be too late to save his grandfather.

Abigail noticed and laid a hand on his shoulder. "We'll get there as quickly as we can," she said.

Andy nodded but said nothing.

As Abigail picked up a long tree branch, which she twirled expertly like a bo staff, Andy glanced down at his Zoomwriter. He twisted the cap, preparing to fire it. The atomic pulse emitter was incredibly powerful, but it could only be used a couple of times before it needed a recharge. He'd have to pick his moment carefully.

Suddenly, Andy remembered a feature on the pen that he'd completely forgotten about. He slapped his head with his palm.

"What is it?" Abigail asked.

"Quick, do you have a piece of paper?"

Abigail nodded and, after a quick search of her rucksack, presented Andy with some. Andy reset his pen to telegraph mode and began to write.

"I forgot that it could do this," Andy murmured as he scribbled a quick note to Ned Lostmore, who would receive the message via Boltonhouse's wireless telegraph.

You're in danger. Don't trust anyone, especially Cedric. On our way to help!

Just knowing that he'd sent his grandfather a warning gave Andy great comfort. He only hoped that it wouldn't arrive too late for Ned to act on it.

"We should aim for that seaplane over there," Rusty said. "Most of the Collective is focused on the main ship where they're loading their gear. If we get a distraction going in the forest behind them, the rest of us can make a beeline for the plane."

Betty and Dotty nodded. "We'll do it. If all goes well, we can meet you upriver."

It sounded to Andy like a good plan. But just in case things got messy, he twisted the cap on his Zoomwriter, setting it back to weapon mode.

While the twins snuck away to a spot where they could surprise the Potentate's crew, Rusty squinted through the bushes at the thugs nearest to them.

Suddenly, a loud crash sounded from the spot Betty and Dotty had chosen to distract the crew. The entire company of thugs shouted and began to point to where Betty and Dotty were hiding.

"Ready?" Rusty said. "One, two, three . . . GO!"

Andy, Abigail, and Rusty sprinted for the seaplane.

At first, it seemed like they were home free. As far as Andy could see, there were no guards in sight. They were all preoccupied with the diversion the twins had caused. But as they closed in on the plane, two guards, clad all in black, leapt out from behind a couple of trees, weapons drawn.

"Get down!" Rusty barked as several razor-sharp throwing knives were hurled in their direction.

Andy and Abigail automatically ducked. Rusty fired at the guards with his pistol, howling like an enraged animal.

One of the guards went down, but the other evaded Rusty's shots and returned fire.

Suddenly, Rusty grabbed his leg and crashed to the ground. "I'm hit!" he yelled.

"Rusty!" Abigail shouted.

Andy responded quickly, pointing his Zoomwriter at the thug and pushing down as hard as he could on the cap.

BOOOOM!

The pulse that flew from the pen shot toward the attacker, knocking him backward about fifty feet through the air. The thug had a wide-eyed expression as he flew, evidently surprised by Andy's attack.

At the sound of his atomic pulse emitter, every eye turned in Andy's direction. Betty and Dotty emerged from the nearby trees and launched themselves at the crowd, spinning like a tornado and singing their fight song.

Now that the Collective had seen what was going on, they mobilized quickly. "Get them!" someone shouted.

The next thing Andy knew, a crowd of about a hundred thugs was bearing down on them. Fear filled his bones. It would be so easy to run away, to leave his companions behind like he had Jack McGraw. But a lot had changed in him since then.

This time, he knew exactly what to do.

"Get to the plane!" Rusty roared.

"I'm not leaving without you!" Andy returned. "Abigail, grab his other arm!"

"Cogs and cornflakes!" Rusty swore. "Let me go! I'll just slow you down!"

Andy leveled a stare at Rusty. "First rule of the Jungle Explorers' Society: nobody gets left behind."

Rusty stared back at Andy, his mustache twitching with annoyance. Then, unexpectedly, his ruddy face split into a wide grin.

"Let's get moving, then!"

The three hurried toward the boat as fast as they could. Once they got a stride going, it wasn't unlike the three-legged races Andy ran at school. Andy kept his Zoomwriter at the ready. He was certain that they would be overtaken soon. The plane lay at a tantalizing distance, but the thugs showed no sign of slowing down.

When Andy could see their snarling faces and the whites of their eyes as he glanced back, he wheeled around and fired his pen.

WHOOOOMP!

The front lines of the attackers went crashing back into the others, sending them tumbling like dominoes.

It not only bought Andy and the others the time they needed to get aboard, but also time for someone else.

The eerie battle song of Betty and Dotty rose over the commotion of the disoriented enemy. As Andy helped Rusty aboard the plane, the twins came into view, flipping expertly over a row of thugs and landing gracefully in the middle of the crowd. They kicked, punched, and let loose their throwing stars as they plowed a trough through the enemy lines. They landed on board the plane with Andy and the others just as the first of the Collective troops were remounting their attack.

"Get us out of here!" Abigail yelled.

Rusty, having a piloted a plane much like this before, started the engine and threw it into gear. The plane leapt from its mooring with a roar and began hurtling upstream. It lifted majestically into the air, leaving in its wake a furious mob of Collective soldiers.

Chapter Twenty-Four
Race to the Boathouse

As Rusty piloted the seaplane above the Amazon, Andy informed the others about what he'd found on the Potentate's desk in the treehouse. Looking at the drawing, the Potentate's notes, and the scary symbols on the Doomsday Device, the peril that they were in became apparent to everyone.

Tens of hours and several fuel stops later, Andy's heart thudded in his chest as he finally saw the Jungle Navigation Company boathouse appear through the tops of the trees. Rusty landed in the water and then taxied the seaplane upriver on its pontoons, navigating slowly toward the mooring where the boats were kept.

Rusty swung the plane in a tight circle, edging it close to the docks. As soon as it stopped, Abigail leapt out and tied it off on a large cleat. The boathouse was a ramshackle building of weathered lumber and rickety stairs. A radio blared top-forty big band music, and birds had taken roost in the rafters.

Andy and the others rushed from the plane.

"It's this way!" Andy exclaimed as he ran from the building, hurtling down a nearby path that he'd taken when he and Jack McGraw's group had headed toward the spot where the Key of Fate had been hidden. Part of the mission to find the key had also involved Jack and his friends creating detailed maps of the area.

Andy hoped that even though it had been days earlier, his grandfather and the expedition group might still be there making maps.

It was strange to be running in the opposite direction from the one Andy had run to escape the horde of angry beasts he'd been so afraid of earlier. When he thought about what he'd done before, he felt ashamed.

How could I have been such a coward?

But he didn't have time to dwell on his past. Right now, all that mattered was the present. His legs pumped, taking huge strides as he dashed down the path, all the while ducking low-hanging branches and hurdling any other obstacles in his way.

Andy held his Zoomwriter clutched in his hand as he ran. He was itching to use it on Cedric, to blast him as far away from his grandfather as possible.

When the group finally made it to the clearing where Jack's group had set up camp, all of them were sweating and out of breath. Andy didn't want to rest. He scanned the area, taking in the tree where Jack and his team had been trapped by the rhino and the hut where the gorillas had recently been.

But then he spotted the thing he feared the most. At the edge of the clearing, standing over a broken heap of metal lying on a table, was Cedric. Andy took in the curved knife he held above his head and the numerous bodies crumpled on the ground next to him.

There were other people there, too. Jack McGraw was bound and gagged, and looked battered and bruised. Standing guard over him were six members of the Collective, all heavily armed. The guards were watching Cedric, who seemed to be in the middle of some kind of strange ceremony.

Andy wasted no time. He pointed his Zoomwriter at the group and shouted, "Cedric! Put down the knife!"

He pushed down hard on the cap, but nothing happened.

Cedric, who was wearing his usual tribal mask,

wheeled around at the sound of Andy's voice. The thugs did the same.

"Get the boy!" Cedric shouted.

All six of the thugs rushed at Andy.

Andy stood his ground. He was aware of his friends on either side of him, all standing in solidarity and ready to defend against the attack.

When the clash came, it sounded like a train slamming into the side of a mountain. There were shouts and the ring of metal as Betty's and Dotty's swords clanged against four of the attackers' long knives. One of the other thugs, a big ugly man with a tattered bandana, slammed into Rusty. He might as well have been slamming into concrete. The big bush pilot was as strong as ever, and it quickly became apparent that, even with his injury, he'd lost none of his fighting prowess. He smashed his single mighty fist repeatedly into his heavyset foe in a blur of attacks too quick for the eye to follow.

Another attacker, a woman with a long silver streak

in her hair and a purple scar across her chin, came for Abigail. Andy hesitated, torn between wanting to help Abigail and wanting to rush to the table where Cedric was standing with his knife. Andy had the sickening feeling that the witch doctor was standing over someone he knew and that he was up to something horrible.

He and Abigail exchanged a look, one that told Andy right away that she had the situation under control. And as the two women began an exchange of martial arts moves, Andy rushed toward his traitorous foe.

At the table, Andy's worst fears were realized. There, amid the broken glass and pieces of metal that had once been Boltonhouse, lay the small shrunken head of Ned Lostmore. His face was gray, and Andy feared the worst.

I'm too late. He's killed him!

Cedric turned toward Andy, and the boy noted the leering grin of his tribal mask. He'd never liked the mask, but now its expression seemed to be mocking him, telling him that Cedric had won and that Andy, in spite of his best efforts, had lost.

Angry tears blurred Andy's eyes.

"What have you done to him?" Andy shouted.

Cedric lifted his mask and looked Andy squarely in the eye. Andy noticed that the small man was smiling and looking very satisfied with himself.

"I've given him a dose of nightshade mixed with tanglethorn. It's a poison that's quite deadly under any circumstances, but it has special potency on victims of magical curses like the great Ned Lostmore here."

He lectured Andy as if he were in front of one of his classrooms at Cambridge. "In a few minutes, complete paralysis will set in, and then, after a very painful series of spasms, Ned Lostmore will die right here on the table."

"How could you?" Andy demanded. "He trusted you!"

"Yes, yes, he did," Cedric said. "That was his mistake. I never liked him much, but I played my part well, don't you think?"

Cedric cocked his head and gazed down at Ned, as if proud of his handiwork. It was too much for Andy. Even though his Zoomwriter wasn't charged up yet, he leapt at the foul villain.

As the two fell to the ground, Andy, who had never been much of a fighter, attacked with all his might. It seemed like every bit of rage he possessed had taken over, and he fought blindly, rolling in the dust while slamming his fists into Cedric over and over again.

For the first time in his life, Andy was winning a fight. But it didn't matter. It wasn't even something to be proud of. All he wanted at that moment was for the pain to go away, and to hurt the man who had stolen the most important person in his life from him.

Cedric managed to twist from Andy's grip. As he stood, he turned to Andy. With an evil grin he said, "You're too late, you know. She already has the Key of Fate. Whether you defeat me or not, you'll all die soon enough!"

Then Cedric turned and ran toward the group of

thugs from the Collective, calling for protection. Andy gave chase, still howling with rage.

When Cedric reached the crowd where the fighting was thickest, Andy saw him remove a glittering orb from his pocket and raise it high above his head.

Andy had seen Cedric use his favorite weapon before. He was particularly fond of crafting decorated bombs that resembled Easter eggs. Cedric now held one of these and, seeing what he was about to do, Andy screamed for him to stop.

It all seemed to happen in slow motion. One second Cedric had the egg above his head and the next he slammed it to the ground.

A billowing cloud of smoke filled the air where the egg had landed. There was no explosion, and Andy wondered if perhaps, by some stroke of luck, he and his friends had been spared an untimely demise. Perhaps the explosive was a dud. But the smoke that filled the air was so thick, Andy couldn't see a thing!

Emerging from the smoke, coughing and haggard,

came Abigail. She rushed over to Andy and said, "Are you all right?"

Andy was relieved to see her. He was pretty sure his nose was bleeding from the fight with Cedric, but he was otherwise okay. He felt like crying, but he did his best to hold back the tears.

He nodded and then said, in a choked voice, "He killed my grandfather."

Abigail didn't say anything for a moment. Then, looking back toward the clearing smoke, she said, "We should get out of here while we can. Follow me. Let the others finish the fight."

But Andy didn't move. He stared at Abigail and said, "What did you say?"

"I said, *let's leave!* The others can fend for themselves!"

And then Andy saw the glittering chain around her neck. Abigail didn't wear jewelry. He knew in a flash who it was that stood in front of him.

He drew his Zoomwriter and pointed it at Cedric.

"Nice try," he said, and pushed down hard on the cap.

KABOOOOM! A huge atomic pulse slammed into Cedric, sending him backward through the air. Andy watched as the villain's unconscious body splashed down into a pool of quicksand. As he slowly sank below the surface of the bog, Andy made no move to rescue him.

The traitor had paid the price for his treachery.

Andy glanced back down at the Zoomwriter. He didn't know how it had happened—usually it took a lot longer to recharge. But his grandfather's gift had been there when he needed it, and now he felt the stinging tears he'd been fighting so hard to hold back come rolling down his cheeks.

Andy walked over to the table and gazed down at the dying form of his grandfather. He looked so small and frail without his protective window. Andy noted Ned's bushy white sideburns and wished that his blue eyes, which were nearly always twinkling with suppressed mirth, would open.

But there was nothing he could do to open them and, Andy realized with a pain deep in his heart, they never would again.

Andy wiped his eyes and tried to come up with words to express how he was feeling. His grandfather had done so much for him. When Andy had first met him, Ned had seen potential in him that nobody else had ever seen. He'd believed in Andy and said he possessed the "Lostmore Spirit."

Andy had wanted nothing more than to live up to his grandfather's expectations and be just like him. After working hard trying to come up with the right words to say, all he could manage was a whisper.

"Grandfather, I . . ." he began, shoving his hands in his pockets.

Andy stopped, his eyes growing wide as his hand touched something in his pocket. He drew out a frond of purple aloe, the same miraculous plant that had healed Rusty.

Andy felt like he was in a dream as he moved close

to his grandfather and squeezed a tiny bit of the plant's juice onto his grandfather's tongue. He stared down at him, wondering if there was still any chance at all.

Please . . .

He was aware of several hands on his shoulders. His friends were nearby. All stared down at Ned Lostmore, their leader, each unable to find a single word to say but all feeling exactly the same.

A moment passed.

And then another.

And then, Ned Lostmore's eyes fluttered open and the color returned to his cheeks. He smacked his lips and said in a weak but cheery English accent, "I say, is that purple aloe I taste? Egad, haven't had any of that in years. Makes a wonderful tea, don't you know. Very restorative!"

Andy yelped with glee. He gently hugged his grandfather to his chest and realized, as he did so, that it was the first time the two of them had actually had any physical contact.

Ned's eyes sparkled as Andy set him back down on the table. "Thank you, Grandson," he said. "I can't tell you how proud I am of you."

Andy cried again. But this time, they were happy tears, and he didn't try to hide them.

Epilogue

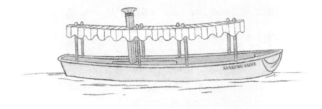

Andy sat on the docks next to his grandfather, relaxing beneath the canopy of twinkling stars that blanketed the sky over the Jungle Navigation Company boathouse. Ned Lostmore had been temporarily installed in a windowed cabinet to protect him until Boltonhouse could be rebuilt, and Andy had wheeled him over to a spot where the two of them could talk in private.

Andy gazed up at the heavens and listened to the

gurgle of the river. "Little Brown Jug," a famous dance tune, played softly on a radio in the background.

"How's Jack McGraw feeling?" Andy asked.

"He's recovering," Ned replied. "He's been through quite a lot."

"I owe him an apology for running away," Andy said.

"Pish posh," said Ned. "He's quite forgotten about that. He saw your loyalty to your friends when you faced off with Cedric and has no doubt about your character."

Andy watched a group of fireflies dancing near one of the Navigation Company boats. The vessel was half submerged in the river, but Andy could see its name, *Sankuru Sadie*, inscribed on the side of the hull. Seeing the broken vessel reminded Andy of his friends and how beaten up they'd been after fighting the Collective.

Ned seemed to read Andy's thoughts and said, "Albert is seeing to it that the others receive proper medical attention. They're safely installed at a very good jungle hospital nearby, a place where I myself worked at one time."

Andy nodded. That was good. But he still felt a bit melancholy. Ned studied Andy, squinting at him through his monocle. "Something bothering you, my boy?"

"We lost the Golden Paw," Andy said. "It sank into the quicksand with Cedric."

"True," Ned said. "And I can think of no better place for it. It's safer there, lost forever, than locked away where someone else can find it."

"When the Potentate was disguised as John Bartlemore, she gave me something called the Ghost Box. I was supposed to put the pendant in it and then the box would vanish, keeping it safe," Andy said.

Ned chuckled. "A great parlor trick, the Ghost Box. But she knew that you would never find the Golden Paw. It was her way of convincing you that she was on the up and up."

Ned bobbed a little on the new string that suspended him in his cabinet. "You can buy those ghost boxes at any magic shop. It's a fairly simple illusion and wouldn't have kept something as dangerous as the Golden Paw any more protected than a cereal box."

Andy was quiet.

"Something else?" Ned asked.

Andy stared off into the shadowy jungle. "Cedric wasn't able to drag the secrets of the Jungle Explorers' Society from you, was he?"

"He tried," Ned said. "But he wasn't prepared for a head such as my own. Quite resistant to torture and the extraction of any information I'm unwilling to give, this noggin of mine." Ned laughed. "I'm always two steps *ahead* of my enemies, don't you know?"

Andy smiled at his grandfather's little joke, but he still felt anxious. "But, Grandfather, Cedric said that the Potentate has the Key of Fate now. If she gets the page from the Library of Alexandria and activates the Doomsday Device, that will be the end of everything. All that we've tried to accomplish, along with our lives, will be lost!"

He looked up at Ned. "I can't stand the idea of losing you again, Grandfather."

Ned chuckled gently. "Nonsense. Don't give up yet, my boy. There are still ways that we can stop her. The last thing you need to learn before becoming a full-fledged member of the Jungle Explorers' Society is that we never give up hope. It's as much a part of who we are as saying yes to adventure and staying loyal to our friends."

Andy sighed. Of all the things he had to learn, perhaps this would be the hardest. It was so easy to think the worst could happen when a terrible situation was staring you in the face. He was a worrier by nature.

"It just so happens that Nicodemus Crumb, an associate of mine, knows the location of a very special person most people don't even know exists. He's older than the oldest trees and incredibly hard to locate. However, I believe that with his help, we still may defeat our enemies."

Andy felt a flicker of hope. He knew his grandfather

well enough to know that if he said there was still a chance, there really was.

"When do we leave?" Andy asked.

"Just as soon as your friends are healed," Ned replied.

Andy gazed at the swirling river, noting how the stars reflected in its surface rippled and moved. It was a beautiful sight, and seeing his reflection there, surrounded by stars, reminded him again of his new friends. He would stick by them through the most difficult of times, and he knew, having seen them in action, that they'd do the same for him.

"Thank you for always being there, Grandfather," Andy said. "For always believing in me, even when I make mistakes."

Ned's blue eyes twinkled as he gazed at his young grandson. "But of course, dear boy. You've got the Lostmore Spirit. And there's nothing you could do that would keep me from believing the best of you."

Andy smiled, and Ned grinned back at him. "Now

then, are you ready for your next adventure? It's bound to be filled with all kinds of danger, excitement, and near-death experiences."

"I *am* a Lostmore," Andy said proudly. "It's what we live for, isn't it?" Then, with a wink, he added the secret word that every Jungle Explorers' Society member said when setting off for adventures.

"Kungaloosh!"